THE CORE

DEAN WESLEY SMITH

Based on the screenplay written by

COOPER LAYNE AND JOHN ROGERS

POCKET BOOKS
New York London Toronto Sydney Singapore

This book is a work of fiction. Names, characters, places and incidents are products of the author's imagination or are used fictitiously. Any resemblance to actual events or locales or persons, living or dead, is entirely coincidental.

An *Original* Publication of POCKET BOOKS

POCKET BOOKS, a division of Simon & Schuster, Inc.
1230 Avenue of the Americas, New York, NY 10020

ISBN: 0-7434-6398-6

First Pocket Books printing March 2003

10 9 8 7 6 5 4 3 2 1

POCKET and colophon are registered trademarks of
Simon & Schuster, Inc.

For information regarding special discounts for bulk purchases,
please contact Simon & Schuster Special Sales at 1-800-456-6798
or business@simonandschuster.com

Printed in the U.S.A.

prologue

DAVID PERRY STARED AT HIS NEW ROLEX, A BIRTHDAY PRESENT from his wife, Tammy, just two days before. It took him a moment of staring at it to understand what he was seeing. "Stopped? Weird," he said to himself.

"You say something, Dave?" Paul asked.

Paul was the only one of the five member team who had stepped into David's office on the way to the board meeting. The others remained in the hallway, waiting for the two of them.

David could feel a tightening in his chest. How could a brand new Rolex stop just minutes before such an important meeting? If he was the superstitious type, he would be worried now.

"Nothing," David said, shaking his head and taking a deep breath. It didn't help the tightening in his chest at all.

His office had a fantastic view of Boston and the Harbor. The city was having one of those beautiful days that made everyone head to the parks, or walk those extra few blocks instead of taking a cab. The sun was warm, but not hot, the humidity low, the wind light.

A perfect day to close one of the biggest deals David and his team had ever tried to pull off. To date David had never landed an account even half the size of the one they were pitching today. And if they landed this one, he would be set for a long time to come.

"We ready, guys?" David asked, smiling at Paul and the three men in the hallway beyond the open door.

"Just waiting for our leader," Paul said, smiling.

David ignored the pain now playing across his chest. The doctor had warned him a year ago when they put his pacemaker in that during times of stress he might feel something like this. If ever there was stress, now was the moment. It was just great to have that heart problem out of the way. It had slowed him down all through his childhood. The pacemaker had given him so much more energy; he couldn't believe it.

"All right," David said, smiling at Paul as he moved around his desk and clasped Paul on the shoulder. "Let's go make thirty million dollars."

The other three members of his team heard that and as a group said, "Yeah!"

Without breaking stride, David entered the hallway, turned and started down the lush corridor, framed with plants and a few doors. The boardroom was only a hundred paces away as David strode forward, focusing on his entrance and his pitch. They had planned to hit the room hard, not really giving the men inside time to get settled in. It was aggressive and would show those in charge that David and his team were in control and capable.

Paul was half a step behind him to his right as planned; the others followed in their positions.

A hard pain in his chest shot up toward David's shoulder, but he ignored it. Nothing was going to stop this sale. Inside that room were the representatives for the third largest conglomerate in the world, and many members of his own company's board. He was going to burst through that door and show them that he and his people had what it was going to take to make this work.

He opened the big double doors, striding forward, just as the pain exploded in his chest. It was as if every system in his body shut down at the same moment.

He managed four more steps, his momentum carrying him facedown onto the big, oak table surrounded by fifteen of the most important people in his business world.

The last thing he thought as the blackness took him was that this was going to be an entrance they would never forget.

*　　*　　*

Directly across the street from the pandemonium in the large boardroom caused by David's entrance, a woman dressed in a tight skirt straddled an older man in the middle of a hallway. The skirt rode up in back, exposing her white underwear, but she didn't care.

The guy on the floor had gray hair, a fairly thin build, and looked to be in good shape. He was the kind of man who normally wouldn't mind a woman in a tight skirt straddling him, except for the fact that he was on his back in the hallway outside his office, unconscious.

The woman, a coworker and his superior from across the hall, pumped his chest, her hands together over his heart. She had taken two classes in CPR when her first husband found out he had a heart condition. She knew what she was doing. A second woman, the man's secretary, had his head tilted back, working in unison with the other woman as she gave him artificial respiration. She too had taken the CPR class.

"Help is on the way?" a third woman said as she emerged from a side office. "What happened?"

The woman straddling the man shook her head. "One moment he was walking along smiling at me, the next he went down."

"Weird," the third woman said.

Below the two office buildings a crowd gathered around two people working over a jogger who had col-

4

lapsed suddenly on the sidewalk. A dozen people who had tried to call for help on their cell phones still puzzled at the fact that the phones wouldn't work.

A half block away a cabby had passed out and ran his cab into a fire hydrant. A cop was working on him, pumping his chest.

In the distance sirens were sounding, responding to dozens of calls in a very small area of the city.

chapter one

"SOUND WAVES GAIN WAVELENGTH AND LOSE FREQUENCY AS they travel through dense materials," Dr. Joshua Keyes said, pointing at one of the large boulders sitting on the demonstration bench, then glanced back over the small audience.

Eighteen students had signed up this semester, actually more than he had expected for an advanced geophysics class. But the eighteen students were dwarfed by the large lecture hall, with tiered seating. It seemed that the University of Illinois only had large lecture rooms.

This one had to have a hundred seats, all anchored to the wooden floor, all with their seats in the up position. The room had high ceilings and a large area in the back, so big that his voice echoed. The entire place smelled of some sort of floor polish, and he could tell the small stage where he stood had been recently waxed, since it looked slick. The people in charge of room assignments had to know that this class never drew enough to even halfway fill this room.

He had been teaching this course now for three years, and this was his largest class yet. And from the looks of the students, the most interested. However, this was the first real day of class, and that interest might change as the semester wore on. For some reason this year the students looked even younger than usual.

As professors went, he wasn't the most conservative, or the most liberal the university had. He taught only three classes and spent the rest of his time on research in his lab. But when he did teach, he liked to involve his students in the classes, entertain them, and speak to them as adults instead of students. He figured at this point in their education, they'd better be interested, or be finding something else to do. But just because they were interested didn't mean he had a license to bore them. So even though the subject was hard, and often dull, he did his best to keep the humor in it.

Around campus he was hard to tell from a student, and was often asked for his student identification. He usually wore jeans and a button-down shirt, sometimes plaid. With his slightly longer hair, at thirty he looked more like a farmhand than a professor.

Today, he had had Acker, his grad student assistant, put three large rocks on the demonstration desk. Acker had told him before class that he had had to draft two football players to help. Josh didn't want to ask how Acker, a tall, skinny nerd of a kid, got football players to help him with anything.

Josh had all three rocks wired up to an oscilloscope with a readout large enough for the entire class to see. This was one of the most basic lectures he would give in this class, yet a needed one. If these students were going to make it to the end of this semester, they had to understand the principles he was going to show them today. Most of them would already know everything he was going to cover, but by coming up with a way to make this lecture entertaining every year, he made sure none of them forgot it.

"The anomalies in low frequency sound waves are the means by which we can surmise the fundamental architecture of our planet."

He patted the boulder, his voice making the oscilloscope needle move a little faster than it had been.

"Allow me to demonstrate," he said. He reached in under the desk and pulled out a trumpet.

A couple of the students laughed, the rest smiled. He was famous around campus as being the worst trumpet player to ever pick up an instrument, and that reputation came mostly from this first basic lecture every year.

Josh pointed to the first boulder. "Now, Mr. Limestone, being the softy he is, loves Miles Davis. Observe how he just sits there and soaks up the sounds."

Josh leaned forward and did his best imitation of a jazz trumpet player. He had taken two years of trumpet lessons when he was seven and eight, and then never touched the instrument again until he started teaching this class. Needless to say, everyone believed that fact.

The oscilloscope needle vibrated wildly, and the students laughed.

Josh stopped, took a slight bow, hamming it up for his audience, then stepped to the next boulder. "Whereas, Mr. Granite, being of rather denser molecular structure, is much less receptive to such fine music."

Again the students laughed.

Josh again did his awful impersonation of Miles Davis. The oscilloscope vibrated much less, but the students laughed even more. Good, they were getting the point.

"Ah, come on Mr. Granite!" he shouted at the boulder, "this is good stuff!"

Josh, playing to the audience, blew even harder into the granite boulder, and the students laughed even louder, some covering their ears.

Then suddenly the only sound in the room was his playing. The students had stopped laughing.

Josh quit and turned to find two men in dark suits striding down through the students toward him. He wanted to blow a note at them to break up the now tense silence, but he didn't. Clearly they were federal agents of some sort. They didn't have a sense of humor.

"What?" Josh asked, "is it a crime to play trumpet to a rock these days?"

A few students snickered.

"Dr. Joshua Keyes?"

Josh glanced at his students and winked. "Mayyy-be."

"Yes or no, sir," the leading agent said, his face showing no signs of humor at all.

"Yes," Josh said.

"Please come with us, sir," the agent said, flashing the FBI badge Josh knew he would be carrying.

"Can't this wait?" Josh asked, indicating the students, all staring in shock.

"Now, sir," the agent said, stopping in front of Josh and indicating that Josh should move toward the door.

"Sorry, gang," Josh said, tossing the trumpet to Acker. "The rock concert will have to be postponed until next class. Acker will get you your assignments."

A couple of the students laughed nervously as Josh stepped out in front of the agent and headed for the door. Acker nodded to him and stood from where he had been sitting off to one side.

Outside the lecture hall, Josh fell in step with the lead agent as they headed down the Earth Sciences building's empty main hallway. Today the place smelled of sulfur and burnt sugar, more than likely from some experiment. Every day this building smelled different.

"Guys, what's going on?"

"We don't know, sir," the agent beside him said.

"You don't know?" Josh asked, actually surprised, looking up at the agent's face. The guy could blend into a crowd and no one would remember him. He had brown eyes, a plain face, and seemed to not even wear an expression.

The agent waited for a student to pass before answering. "Your security clearance is higher than ours, sir."

"Oh, right," Josh said, following the agent out into the warm sun. "I have security clearance."

"We're just here to bring you to your jet, sir," the agent said, pointing down the sidewalk toward an official-looking car parked at the curb.

"Oh," Josh said. Then what the agent had said finally sunk in. "I have a jet?"

The agent said nothing more.

The skyline of Washington, D.C., was stunning in the clear noon sun. In all his times in and out of the nation's capital, Josh never tired of seeing the monuments, the Capitol dome, the White House. It helped him to keep perspective on some of the stakes he had fought for over the years.

Now, for some reason no one seemed to know, they had hustled him out of class in Chicago and onto a very comfortable, unmarked private jet. A steward had served him a quick lunch and a soda, and then offered him magazines to read for the remainder of the hour-long flight. Josh had chosen to just sit and stare out the window. It wasn't often a geophysics professor like him had his own plane. He wanted to enjoy the moment.

A black limo met his plane right on the runway, as two different agents whisked him into the car. Neither of them knew anything either.

Finally, after a quick, police-escorted trip through the D.C. traffic, they pulled into an underground entrance at Bethesda Naval Hospital. Now Josh was really confused. Why would the government take him out of a class to bring him to a hospital?

They passed quickly through two security checks in the basement area, and then went down into the center of the complex, descending at least three more floors.

Guards were everywhere, and guys in Hazmat suits as well, which didn't bode well for what Josh was going to face. He wasn't real thrilled with the idea of going into an area of a hospital where some people thought it necessary to wear those suits.

Then, Josh saw a familiar sight. His old friend, Serge Leveque, stood banging on a soda machine, swearing at it in graphic French. Serge was, without a doubt, the strangest Frenchman in the world of science, and maybe the most brilliant. He and Josh had gotten to know each other over the years, becoming unlikely best friends.

Serge was a heavyset man, and almost always wore a topcoat of some type, no matter what the weather. He had that same dark coat on now, even though it had to be eighty degrees outside. He was about eight years older than Josh, gaining quickly on forty, something Josh had fun not letting him forget. He lived in Washington with his wife and worked on God-knew-what secret weapons projects for the government.

"Serge!" Josh shouted.

Serge turned, grinning. "About time. They would not brief me until you got here."

Serge wrapped Josh in his normal bear hug greeting.

"Any idea what's going on?" Josh asked as the agent led them even farther into the middle of the hospital complex.

"Big panic," Serge said, shrugging. "Biochemists, lots of military. How are you, *mon ami?*"

"Great," Josh said. "Did you know I had a jet?"

"I think they are going to want it back," Serge said, laughing.

"How's the family?" Josh asked as they moved through two more security checkpoints.

Serge waved his hand as if swatting at a fly in front of his face. "Madeleine is well, but the children have become foul American brats. They like Burger King and cartoons and have forsaken all French culture."

Josh laughed. "Who can blame them?"

The agent kept leading them deeper into an area of the hospital that Josh had no doubt very few people had ever entered. The halls were a dull gray, the floors smooth and polished, the soldiers stone-faced and posted at every intersection. Some of the halls even smelled musty, as if they were seldom used.

"When are you going to meet a nice girl?" Serge asked. "Bring her to dinner?"

Josh shrugged. At this point in his life, the last thing he was interested in was women. He barely had time to prepare for classes and do his research.

"Ahh, married to your work, eh?" Serge said, almost as if reading his thoughts. "Good, so am I, which makes my wife my mistress." He laughed in only the way Serge could laugh, his body shaking, the sound echoing powerfully through the halls. "That's why I'm still in love with her."

At that moment the agent took them through a set

15

of double doors and into a room full of gurneys covered in white sheets. The place had a low ceiling and smelled of some sort of cleaning solution. And something else that Josh couldn't put his finger on.

He squinted, letting his eyes adjust to the dimmer light. It took him a moment to realize what he was seeing.

"Fuck, those are bodies!"

"We have taken a wrong turn," Serge said, backing toward the door that had now closed.

"No," a man said from behind them, "if you had taken a wrong turn, you would have already been shot."

Both Josh and Serge turned around.

Josh studied the man standing there. He was a three-star general, about fifty, with typical military posture and a hard intelligence in his eyes that Josh had not often seen in the military types.

"Hello to you too, *mon général,*" Serge said.

"Serge," the general said, "always a pleasure."

Josh could tell that the two had clearly had a few meetings in the past. And from the way Serge acted, not always good meetings.

The general turned and nodded to the agent who had led them there. He snapped around and left, pulling the door closed behind him, leaving the three of them alone in the room full of bodies.

No matter how many scenarios Josh could have imagined for reasons the government needed to fly him to Washington, D.C., standing in a room full of bodies was not it. He wouldn't have driven downtown if he knew this was where he was going to end up, even at gunpoint.

As the door closed, the general turned, smiling and extending his hand. "Dr. Keyes, Thomas Purcell."

Josh hoped he managed to hide his surprise. General Thomas Purcell was one of the most powerful men in all the military. If he was the one that called Josh here, it was no wonder Josh suddenly had a jet. It also meant that whatever was going on it was big-time stuff.

"As you probably realize," the general said, jumping right to the topic at hand, "what you're about to hear is highly classified."

Both Josh and Serge nodded, so the general went on before Josh could ask for a slightly better meeting room. One with a few less dead people.

"At ten-thirty A.M., local time, seventeen civilians, all within a three-block radius, died. They did not get sick first. They simply hit the ground, dead."

The general pointed at the gurneys covered with bodies and white sheets.

Josh stared at the corpses spread out in front of him. So this morning all these people had been alive, leading normal lives, with jobs and families and friends. Now he really was going to be sick. There was a reason he studied magnetism and rocks instead of animals and humans.

"Bioweapon?" Serge asked.

"Our first guess," the general said, "but no."

Josh was glad to hear that, up to a point. He tried to focus on the task at hand. "They all died at the same time?"

"As far as we can tell, to the second," the general said.

Josh instantly knew what had happened, and now half-wished it had been a bioweapon.

"This hits CNN in one hour," the general said, staring first at Josh, then at Serge. "I need a reason."

"Variation in sex, age, body types?" Serge asked, clearly trying to make some sense out of the information.

"They all had pacemakers," Josh stated.

Serge turned to stare at Josh.

General Purcell chuckled and glanced at his watch. "Under one minute. Your reputation is well deserved, Dr. Keyes."

Josh didn't know he had a reputation in the circles that General Purcell moved in. He'd have to give that some thought.

The general moved over and pulled the sheet back from one of the victims. The man had been fairly young, not more than forty. He had a stylish, businesslike haircut. The heart operation scar ran down the center of his chest, red and angry-looking on his deathly white skin.

"Hey, hey," Josh said, looking away, forcing the lunch he had been served on the plane to stay in place. The last thing he needed was to stare at a bunch of dead bodies. He would have nightmares for a month as it was just being in this room.

"How did you guess?" the general asked, "with no clues from the victims?"

The general covered up the body as Josh answered. "Serge and I are the clue."

The general looked puzzled, so Josh went on. "Serge specializes in high energy weapons. I do geomagnetics. So calling us means you suspect an electromagnetic pulse weapon. If these are the only fatalities, they must be people susceptible to electromagnetic interference."

"Thus pacemakers," Serge said, shaking his head. "Sometimes you are spooky, my friend."

"Now I need to know if some sort of weapon killed these people," the general said.

"Three-block radius?" Josh asked.

The general nodded.

Josh worked to compute the amount of energy it would take to cover an area of that size. It would have to have been a very large amount.

"Any tremors detected from a detonation?" Serge asked before Josh could.

"No," the general said.

"Too much power," Josh said. He didn't say that it would take a small nuke to generate that kind of EM blast, powerful enough to shut off pacemakers in a three-block area.

Serge nodded. "I agree. Too much."

"It's no weapon I've ever heard of," Josh said.

"He is right, General."

"You're not seeing an EM pulse weapon here?" the general asked, his gaze intent on Josh, then on Serge.

Both shook their heads no.

"Thank you," the general said, indicating they should head for the door. "We're done here."

"We're not done," Josh said, stunned at the general's sudden action. "There's nothing on the other side of the equal sign."

"I agree with Josh," Serge said. "Something caused this."

Josh had a few ideas of what it might have been, but he needed far more information.

The general stopped at the door and faced the two scientists. Josh could see the intensity in his eyes, the focus, and the relief. "Our greatest concern, was that this may have been an act of war. As long as it's not, we can all breathe a little easier, can't we?" He turned and pushed open the doorway, nodding to the agent there.

Serge and Josh followed him into the hallway. The

quicker Josh got away from those bodies, the happier he would be. But he didn't want to leave everything yet. The general had given him a puzzle; he had answered a question. But there were a thousand more questions that needed answering.

"Thank you, gentlemen," the general said, then turned and strode off as the agent indicated Serge and Josh should go in another direction.

Josh glanced back at the seventeen bodies on the gurneys filling the room just before the door swung closed. He had no doubt that he was not going to breathe easier, as the general had said, any time soon.

Or sleep well, either. Not with this many unanswered questions.

chapter two

THE KID STARTED CRYING, POINTING TO SOMETHING THAT LAY on the ground in Trafalgar Square. It was a beautiful day, in the low sixties, with almost no wind or clouds in the sky. His parents, both from San Francisco, didn't notice their child's discomfort for a moment. The kid kept crying until finally the mother bent down to talk to him.

"What is it, sweetheart?"

The boy pointed to a dead bird lying on the stone surface among dozens of other live birds.

The mother nodded, patted the boy's cheek, and stood, indicating that her husband should talk to their son.

"Well, Sam," the father said, bending down to face his son, "that happens sometimes. The birdie is flying and—"

Another dead pigeon landed not more than a yard from them with a sickening thump, bouncing slightly on the stone surface of the square.

The boy started crying even harder, holding onto his mother's leg.

Two more dead birds fell from the sky.

Then suddenly all the birds were in flight, thousands and thousands of pigeons, all seeming to fly in all directions at once, seeming not to care where they were going.

The tourists filling the square started shouting.

A woman screamed as a bird got caught in her hair.

A man lost an eye as a bird flew right into his face.

The father, stunned, looked up at the swarming birds. They seemed to be everywhere, smashing into buildings, each other, people, cars. A window shattered to the family's right, then another and another.

"Let's go!" the mother shouted to her husband. She picked up her crying son and started to run with the rest of the panicked mob.

The birds were everywhere, like a scene from the old Hitchcock movie, filling the sky with panic that only fueled the human panic on the ground.

The sound of the kid's cry as a bird slammed into him and knocked him out of his mother's arms was lost in the chorus of shouts, breaking glass, and bird screams.

His mother screamed, fought her way against the surging crowd to find her son, who had vanished in the mob.

Birds cut at her face, smashed into her shoulder.

A man rammed his shoulder into her.

Her husband was nowhere to be seen.

She tripped on someone and fell to the ground, scraping her knees on the stone, but somehow she managed to get back up.

The panic filled her, giving her energy to claw and fight her way through the human and bird panic back to where she had lost her son.

Finally she found him. He had been trampled and lay bleeding among the dead birds, his arms twisted, his back broken, just as if he too had fallen from the sky.

Josh didn't much notice the flight to Chicago, and the short ride back to the University of Illinois. He had stayed completely engrossed in how seventeen pacemakers could quit all at once. The puzzle at least kept his mind off the room full of dead bodies, and the attendant smell.

He wished he had more information about what else had quit around those victims. The general had said it had been a three-block radius. If something had stopped that many pacemakers, it had stopped other things as well. But Josh didn't know what, or for that matter, even what city it had happened in.

He'd made a few phone calls from the plane trying to get more information, then gave up. It seemed that so far no one he knew was inside the loop on this thing.

Finally back on campus, he headed for his office, which adjoined his research lab. As he entered the lab his two graduate assistants looked up, then smiled. Acker, a twenty-two-year-old, brilliant doctoral student, had been in class helping with the demo the day before, when the federal agents whisked Josh away. If there was anyone with a bigger mouth in all the physics department, then it was the skinny, long-haired Acker.

Josh's other grad student assistant was Danni, a bright, red-haired twenty-three-year-old who had more boy problems than anyone Josh had ever known. Next to Acker, she was the best graduate assistant he had ever had. Both were already good scientists. Someday they might even become great ones.

"He's a man who lives a life of danger . . ." Acker sang as Josh entered.

Danni glanced up from the project she was working on. "What did the Men in Black want?"

"If he told us," Acker said, laughing, "they'd have to shoot us. Right?"

"Anything on the news about pacemakers?" Josh asked, ignoring both of them as he got himself a can of pop cooled by an experiment they were working on with liquid nitrogen.

"Yeah," Danni said. Something about a manufacturers' defect but it got pushed off by the birds."

"Birds?" Josh asked, heading for the small television set they had in a corner of the lab. It was surrounded by a very comfortable couch, an old coffee table covered in soda cans, and two chairs. He had spent far, far too much time in that area over the years. He'd even slept on the couch more times than he wanted to count.

His two assistants joined him, and Acker flipped on the TV.

A BBC reporter stood in the middle of what looked like a war zone. Around him was clearly Trafalgar Square, but it looked as if a bomb had gone off. Broken windows, emergency vehicles, everything.

And thousands and thousands of dead birds littering the ground.

"Eleven people are confirmed dead," the reporter said. "Trampled in the panic. Eyewitnesses state the swarming birds were not actually attacking people, but seemed to be flying blind."

"Weird," Josh said, trying to wrap his mind around something like that at the same time as thinking about what he saw in Washington.

"Weird indeed," Acker said. "And it's not the first time, you know."

Josh knew that Acker's hobby was conspiracy. He subscribed to every known conspiracy magazine, bought every Charles Fort book, and knew far too much about the behind-the-scenes activities of the CIA than any average citizen should ever know.

But right now Josh figured that Acker's crazy hobby just might help him. "When were the last ones?"

Acker smiled. "If I remember right, there were violent bird swarms last month in both Australia and Japan."

"How do birds navigate?" Josh asked, almost afraid of the answer he guessed might be the case.

"Sight," Danni said.

"No, I mean the long range stuff."

"Magnetic field," Danni said. "Little ions in their brains align with the magnetic field of the Earth."

Suddenly everything seemed to click into place. The magnetic field of the entire planet just might be shifting. If what he was thinking was right, they were all in big trouble.

Josh shook his head. At the moment he didn't have enough information to jump to such a conclusion. Before he even mentioned the idea to anyone, he had to have some proof.

He turned and headed for the blackboard at the end of the room near his office. Quickly he erased it, then while writing spoke to the two grad students who had followed him.

"Acker, hit the Net, do a two-year search for any and all, oh, weird news."

He quickly listed on the board the areas he wanted searched for as he spoke. "Bizarre animal migrations, specifically birds. Dolphin and whale beachings. Unusual atmospheric phenomena, unexplained air crashes. Use your imagination, but list them up here as you go."

"That's a huge search," Acker said.

"You're up to this," Josh said. "Use the T-1 line and get help from the computer department where you need it."

Acker nodded. Josh turned to Danni.

"Get the brightest kids from the Field Theory class and have them design a computer model of an electromagnetic field."

"What are we doing?" Danni asked.

"I need a 3-D computer model of the Earth to lay the field over," Josh said.

"The planet Earth?" Danni asked, shocked.

"Yeah," Josh said, smiling at her, "you know, the pretty blue one."

She stuck out her tongue at him, so he went on.

"I need you to map out the anomalies Acker finds, to grunt out the equations. Grab those smelly kids from the Non-linear Differential class."

He saw befuddled looks on both their faces. "Do this

and I'll sign your doctorates blindfolded. Do not pass Go, go directly to Ph.D."

Acker stood there for a moment, then with a glance at Danni, he turned and ran toward the computer area of the lab. Danni wasn't more than a half step behind him as she went out the door.

"Be wrong, be wrong, be wrong," Josh said to himself, turning and heading into his office. If the magnetic field of this planet was shifting, everyone on Earth was in for some very ugly, and possibly terminal, times ahead.

Major Rebecca "Beck" Childs sat in *Endeavor*'s copilot seat, her grip light on the control stick. At twenty-nine, she looked younger than her years, and had a model's face. She often used that look to her advantage when someone thought she should be walking a fashion runway instead of working to be the best pilot in the Air Force.

And in space.

So far this shuttle mission had lasted for five days. Five wonderful days of weightlessness, careful work, and fantastic views. There was no way she would ever get tired of the view of the Earth's surface and white clouds speeding past.

"We are in attitude and ready for entry interface," she reported as *Endeavor* finished its rotation on its long axis and she eased it to a stop. The butterflies in her stomach were pounding to be let out, but she didn't let anyone know that. Every time she got a chance to fly a shuttle, even for a simple staging move, she was happy.

"Nice work, Major," Mission Commander Robert Iverson said, glancing over the readouts. He was forty and ex-navy. He looked the pilot type, with the standard strong jaw and dry sense of humor. "I have the controls now for *E. I.*"

"I could take us in," Beck said, keeping her hands on the stick.

Behind them flight engineer Timmins laughed, but said nothing.

"You could," Iverson said, smiling at her. "But you won't."

"I'm ready for this, Bob," she said. She had been talking about getting the chance to land the shuttle for some time now, ever since her first mission two years ago. Maybe today, if Iverson was feeling up to it, might be the day.

"No, you are not, Beck," Iverson said. "You are trained, you are certified; that does not make you the commander. And the commander lands the bird."

He glanced at her and smiled. "You got to be the youngest person ever in space. Say thank you and be happy."

"Okay, for now." Beck lifted her hands off the controls as Iverson took over. What she didn't say was that maybe next time she would be the commander. She planned on being back up here a lot over the coming years.

"*Endeavor*, Houston, at this time we show you go for re-entry."

The voice was Talma "Stick" Stickley, NASA Control Chief and an iron fist in a smooth, southern drawl. Beck liked her a great deal. Stick had done a lot to help get Beck into space as early as she had.

"Houston, *Endeavor* coming up on entry interface," Beck said, reading off the instruments as Iverson focused on the flying.

"*Endeavor*, this is Flight," Stick said, her voice clearly showing humor. "Weren't you able to annoy the commander into letting you bring her in this time?"

Beck managed to not laugh. "Negative, Stick. I'll have to be more annoying next time."

"Is that even possible?" Iverson asked under his breath beside her.

"*Endeavor*," Stick said, "we see you in a good entry config."

"Roger, Houston," Beck said.

Now there was no more joking around. Getting this big bird slowed down enough to let them land without burning to a cinder was the most dangerous part of the mission.

Beck let her gaze dart from one readout to another as around them the shuttle bounced and began to heat up as it hit the upper atmosphere. Outside the windows the blackness of space turned orange as the high, thin part of the atmosphere heated up the tiles on *Endeavor*'s skin.

The seconds ticked past as no one said a word. All instruments read green. They were in the chute and tracking.

Commander Iverson seemed the coolest, most controlled person Beck had ever seen, even as he fought to keep *Endeavor* on course and steady through the bouncing of the reentry.

Then, almost as quickly as it started, the heat around the shuttle was gone and they were now a glider, falling like a rock, but a glider nonetheless.

Beck let out a sigh of relief, and beside her she could see Iverson relax as well.

"Endeavor," Stick's voice said, calm as always, "y'all have deviated from course. Verify your flight control is in auto."

Beck glanced at Iverson, who was frowning, then did as Stick had asked. "Houston, affirmative. Nav looks good to us. Everything showing green."

Iverson loosed his lap belt a little and pushed himself up enough to look out the window, then back at his instruments. "We're out of position here."

"Guidance shows us on course," Timmins said from behind Beck.

Beck clamped down on the fear inside her, making herself remain cool and thinking. But if they had deviated from course by too far, they were in big, big trouble.

"I've made this approach two hundred and thirteen times in the simulator," Iverson said. "We're not where we should be."

"Then were the hell are we?" Beck demanded, yanking out a laminated map board and wax pencil. She strained against her belt to look out the window. What she saw could not be possible. "Is that a city?"

There were no cities anywhere near their entry path. Considering the sonic concussions that they generated coming in, there didn't dare be a city close by.

"*Endeavor*," Stick said, "guidance is bad. You are now one-niner-two miles off course."

Not possible! Beck wanted to shout, but she did not. How could the shuttle come in almost two hundred miles off course? That wasn't possible.

"Roger, Houston," Beck said, "we sort of noticed that. "Is that—"

"Los Angeles," Stick said. "That is confirmed."

"We're at one five thousand feet," Iverson said. "We've got maybe two minutes of glide time left."

"We're heading right for downtown," Beck said.

"We're not going to crash into Los Angeles," Iverson said.

Mission control in Houston was scrambling for ideas. "Decrease the descent angle, maybe they can swing toward the desert," a chief engineer suggested.

Stick shook her head.

"The more they turn, the faster they fall. They'll never clear the LA Basin. Can they make the airport?"

"Five miles short," the engineer said.

Beck could not believe the death sentence they had just been handed. How could a computer flight insertion be that far wrong? None of this should be happening. But it was, and there had to be a way to save them, and this bird, and who knows how many people on the ground.

"I'm trying to increase our glide time," Iverson reported, fighting the stick.

Beck knew what he was thinking. Maybe, if he held the ship in a perfect angle, he could gain those five miles. She doubted it, but it was the right thing for him to try at the moment.

She yanked out her battered flight case and pulled out her pilot's navigational aid. They were going to fall short of the airport, but maybe a freeway.

Clearly Iverson was thinking the same thing.

"Houston, those buildings are getting mighty big down there. Can you clear a freeway?"

"Rush hour, commander," Stick said.

Suddenly Beck knew where they needed to set down. Fortunately at that time of year, the conduit for the Los Angeles River was dry. With some fancy flying, they just might make it. "I found us an alternate. If we turn to heading one-eight-zero."

"That's Houston's call," Iverson said. "Houston?"

"Computers are still plotting," Stick said.

"Sir," Beck said, trying to get through to the commander. "I have an alternate."

"Houston, we're running out of time up here," Iverson said, ignoring her.

"Houston," Beck said, finishing the work on her pad that she needed to confirm her idea. "I have a vector for an alternate landing site. Can you confirm?"

"*Endeavor*," Stick said, "give 'em to me."

"I show a possible touchdown at thirty-five degrees, forty minutes north, eighty-four degrees, twenty-two minutes west."

There was the longest pause Beck could ever remember. Below, the city seemed to be coming up at them at with alarming speed. They didn't have much time. Someone had to make a decision, or they were just going to plow through neighborhoods, schools, and who knew what else.

"*Endeavor*," Stick said, "you have got a set of brass ones. That is confirmed. Take CSS and head for your field. We'll call ahead."

"Say again, Houston?" Iverson asked, clearly not understanding what had just happened.

"*Endeavor,* turn right," Stick said, "heading one-eight-zero."

Iverson automatically followed instructions, easing the shuttle onto its new course, conserving all the speed and air time he could.

"Expect visual contact with the Los Angeles River in thirty seconds."

"This won't work, Houston," Iverson said, glancing at Beck. "We've got bridges every few hundred yards. "Our wingspan alone is going to—"

"Sir," Beck said, "I've figured the ratios. We can make it if you bring us straight in."

Iverson nodded and made the slight change in heading.

"We are coming in high and hot," Timmins said from behind her. Clearly he too had already figured out the details for the new landing sight.

Ahead of them the river stretched, wide and empty through the city, a band of concrete that no one in their right mind would ever think to use as a landing strip.

At the moment they weren't in their right mind. They just didn't have a choice.

"Call it out!" Iverson said.

Beck took a deep breath and forced herself to take

her eyes away from the sight ahead and stare at the altitude and speed. "Two hundred and ninety feet, three hundred and twenty."

She paused as Iverson kept the big bird level.

"Two hundred and seventy feet," she said. "Three-oh-five."

"Gear down now!" Iverson ordered.

Beck snapped the lever, lowering the landing gear. She heard it lock into place and saw the lights change to green.

"Down and locked," she said.

She knew that was way too fast, but at this point they had no choice at all, with anything. She could just imagine what the sonic impact had done to buildings they had passed over before they dropped under the speed of sound.

"Close!" Timmins said, as the shuttle somehow managed to skim over a bridge and drop hard onto the concrete of the river basin.

Beck was impressed. Iverson had got them in dead center.

"Bringing the nose down," Iverson said, dropping it just in time as they flashed under a bridge.

Beck knew that if he had waited a second longer they would have smashed into that bridge, nose up. Yet with the nose down the shuttle fit under the bridge.

Beck hit the speed brakes, yanking them open far

faster than she should have. But their ground speed was still far too fast. "Two-thirty," she read off. "Two-twenty. Two-ten."

"Deploy the drag chutes," Timmons said behind her.

Beck made no move to do so.

"No," Iverson said. "We snag a bridge and we'll tear the tail off."

"Uh, oh," Beck said, staring ahead at the next bridge. It was divided into three sections. And low. Cockpit level.

"Pull the gear!" Beck said, reaching for it.

"Not yet," Iverson said. "We'll lose all steering."

She held her hand over the lever, waiting for the commander's orders. The bridge was coming up at them faster than she could ever have thought possible. Their ground speed was still over two hundred miles per hour and if she didn't drop that gear at the right moment, she was going to slam face first into that concrete slab.

"Do it!" Iverson shouted.

Beck hit the series of levers that dropped the gear. Under them the landing gear gave way and the shuttle dropped to concrete, bouncing them around as it slid forward.

Iverson had them on target and they slid under the bridge, shearing off the tip of the tail.

Now there was nothing they could do but hang on

and hope. Ahead scaffolding covered the next bridge, built up from the river bottom. There had to be a half dozen workers on that scaffolding. Beck could only imagine what it must be like for them to have a shuttle sliding at them on its belly. Not something you would go to work in the morning expecting to happen.

And not a good way to die.

They were slowing quickly, the sound of metal scraping concrete was worse than anything Beck had ever heard.

And the shaking was worse than in the upper levels of the atmosphere.

Just when she was convinced the shuttle was going to slide into the helpless men, frozen, watching them from the scaffolding, they came to a stop.

Feet to spare.

The silence overwhelmed the cabin. Never had Beck imagined that silence could sound so wonderful. They were down and no one had died.

Iverson let out a long, deep sigh.

Beck glanced over at him. "We took the collision insurance, right?"

Timmons laughed, but all Iverson could do was glare at her.

chapter three

THE LAST FEW DAYS IN THE GEOPHYSICS LAB HAD BEEN THE MOST intense Josh had ever lived. Every fiber of his being was focused on trying to prove his own theory wrong. He desperately wanted the Earth's magnetic field to be stable, not be shifting.

Yet the more details they plotted in, the more weird events Acker found, the more equations Josh ran, the more he was convinced his first conclusion had been only partially right. What really was happening was far, far worse.

Now, he had one final program to run, one final test.

The lab was empty, with Acker and Danni off getting dinner.

He double-checked that the data had been fed into the computer correctly, then hit the Start key. The image of the Earth on the screen rotated slowly as one pattern after another was overlaid on the image, one calculation after another figured and plotted in. Each pattern, each layer on the image was a different color, indicating a different variable.

He watched as the computer built the model of what was going to happen over the next few days, then weeks, and when it was finally done a single word flashed on the screen.

"Not possible," he said, banging the keyboard with one hand. Then he quickly reset everything, spent twenty minutes checking the data again, and then ran the program again.

Same conclusion.

The word Terminal blinked over the image of the planet Earth.

If he was right, if this program was right, if all his calculations were right, none of them stood a chance. The human race would be gone sooner than anyone had ever thought possible.

Suddenly the door to the lab broke open and Danni and Acker rushed in.

"Turn on the news!" Danni shouted. "The news. The shuttle—"

"Danni," Josh said, his voice soft. He turned so his back covered the results of the computer simulation on the screen.

Both Acker and Danni stopped short.

"The shuttle," Acker said, pointing to the television.

"Danni," Josh said, ignoring Acker's insistence that he turn on the TV. He needed to add one more data point into the calculations that would avoid dooming the planet. "Acker's had a mad crush on you for a year."

"Doc!" Acker said. His face turned red and he stared at the floor.

Danni looked at Acker, then back at Josh, clearly puzzled.

Josh turned to Acker. "Danni's had a mad crush on you for eight months."

Now Acker and Danni both stared at each other, neither knowing what to say. That had to be a first for both of them.

Josh reached into his wallet and pulled out a credit card. "This is my credit card," he said, handing the card to Acker. "Go to the Four Seasons. Get a suite. Order champagne."

"Doc?" Acker said, "Are you all right?"

"You've both worked hard, take the time, spend the money, get to know each other."

Acker glanced at the card. Then they both nodded and slowly, as if not sure what had just happened, headed back out, pulling the door closed behind them.

Josh turned to the big screen, staring at the computer generated model of the planet Earth, its magnetic fields, and the repercussions of what was happening. The word Terminal just kept flashing over the image.

Slowly he slid down to sit on the floor. "Don't make me the one," he said to himself.

But he knew he was the one.

He was going to have to tell the entire human race it was doomed. And at this point he doubted anyone would listen.

The flight to Washington this time was a lot different than his last trip. He had booked a regular ticket the night before, and then barely made the flight with the folder and copies of his calculations, ending up sitting between a man who snored the entire flight and a woman who wanted to talk.

The reason for this trip was that he had to have some backup on what he had found, and the only person he could think of to help him was the famous Dr. Conrad Zimsky, who just happened to be speaking at the Smithsonian that afternoon. Zimsky considered himself the leading brain in many fields, including geophysics. Josh wasn't so sure what exactly Zimsky was leading in except great hype, but at the moment Zimsky was the only one Josh could think of who had the brains and the background to verify Josh's calculations. And he doubted Zimsky would help.

But at least Josh had to try.

Josh made it across the city just in time to catch the last few minutes of Zimsky's speech. He positioned himself in such a fashion that he was between Zimsky and the waiting limousine, standing at the top of a staircase that Zimsky would have to go down to leave.

Zimsky finished his speech, took a few bows to the applause, and then with a mob of people around him, headed toward the stairs and Josh.

Zimsky looked the part of a famous genius, with unruly hair, baggy clothes, and a large nose that held glasses halfway down. Almost a clichéd mad scientist look. Josh had no doubt it was all done for the media.

"Dr. Zimsky," Josh shouted as he elbowed his way close to the scientist, "My name is Josh Keyes."

Josh handed him the folder, and Zimsky started to autograph it, as if someone had thrust him a picture to sign.

"No, I need you to look those papers over," Josh said, as Zimsky handed him the folder back, now signed.

"Glad to meet you," Zimsky said, clearly on autopilot and trying to get to his limo. "Now pardon me, I'm late for the White House."

He headed down the stairs as Josh followed, staying right with the man.

"Don't sign it," Josh said, his voice hard and firm as he thrust the folder back at Zimsky. "Read it. I need you to confirm my results."

Zimsky hit the bottom of the stairs with Josh right beside him. He stopped, clearly annoyed and turned to face Josh, shoving the folder back. "Do you have any idea who I am?"

"Yes," Josh said, "I do. Now read it."

Josh pushed the folder back at Zimsky without taking it.

"What is it?" Zimsky demanded.

"The end of the world," Josh said.

That froze Zimsky. Then the famous scientist laughed.

Josh did not.

After a moment Zimsky stopped as well, then, even with the people flowing around them, waiting for him to pay them even the slightest attention, Zimsky's curiosity got the better of him. He opened the folder and glanced at the first page.

Then he flipped through a few other pages and closed the folder.

He looked Josh in the eye. "Come with me."

Two hours later, in Zimsky's office, Josh was pacing in front of the man's desk, hoping against all hope that his figures were wrong. And if anyone could find where he had made a mistake, it was Zimsky.

The office was the kind of place Josh would expect from a famous scientist who believed his own hype. It had oak desks, oak shelves, and more books than most libraries in this and adjoining rooms. It also had a couch and a usable white-board that Zimsky clearly often used. But the office was too clean to be a real working scientist's office.

For two hours Zimsky had been alternating from reading Josh's pages, and working on the white board, checking calculations.

Finally Zimsky dropped back into his chair and looked up at Josh.

"Shit!" Josh said, falling into a chair across the desk. He knew Zimsky had proven his calculations were right, just from the look on the man's face.

"No," Zimsky said, banging the papers on the desk, "there's no way I missed this. You must be wrong."

"Arrogance as scientific principle," Josh said, shaking his head in disgust. "Great."

Zimsky glared at him. "I'm sure you're the best in your field."

"Geophysics," Josh said.

"Then you're not the best," Zimsky said.

"I know," Josh said. "But this combines geophysics and electromagnetic field theory, so—"

"And your doctorate is in?" Zimsky asked, feeling smug.

"Both," Josh said.

Zimsky actually had the common sense to frown. This clearly was not the joke he had hoped it might be.

"I'm sure with careful comparison to my own work," Zimsky said, "we'll find you're mistaken."

"We'll know soon enough," Josh said, standing and turning away. "The bigger effects will start up any day now."

Josh grabbed the door and yanked it open.

"Where are you going?" Zimsky demanded, obviously not used to someone walking out on him.

"Just got to keep moving," Josh said, slamming the door behind him as he left. There was no chance he was going to get any more help out of that arrogant bastard. And since his calculations were right, it didn't matter anyway. Mankind was doomed.

And the best thing he could think to do about it was get drunk.

Major Beck Childs strode out of the Pentagon office and almost smack into General Purcell. She had been hanging around, meeting with whomever would talk with her about the accident. She needed to know how it was going to come down, and so far no one was doing much talking, even though her entire life depended on it.

The investigation into the shuttle crash had yet to really begin, but the preliminary findings were that it had been a guidance system malfunction of some sort. Beyond that, if Commander Iverson or she got blamed, was anyone's guess.

"Rebecca," General Purcell said, extending his hand.

Beck took the offered hand and shook it warmly. The general had been a friend of the family for years. Some of her earliest memories were of him with her father.

"Only you and Dad ever call me that," she said, smiling.

"Sorry," the general said, laughing. "Beck."

She turned and headed in the direction he had been going, toward one of the main doors.

"So what brings you to sunny D.C.?" he asked.

"The Board of Review is next week," she said, watching for his reaction.

He just kept walking, nodding.

"I'm just trying to get a sense of the mood upstairs."

"Makes sense," he said.

"How bad is it?" she asked him flat out, shocked that she had pushed so directly.

The general shook his head, stopped, and faced her. "Beck, your crew crashed the space shuttle. How good do you think it could be?"

"Sir, this is my life," she said. "I was studying for the Academy when I was thirteen. It has always been, and still is, my whole damn life."

"It's over," he said, his eyes full of sadness, but clear. His words were firm.

She just stared at him. She couldn't believe what he had just said. How could it be over?

"It's over, Rebecca," he said. "I'm sorry."

She wanted to scream at him, hit him, pound him into a pulp for even thinking such thoughts. But instead she just stood there, staring at him, too numb to even move.

Suddenly almost a dozen people rushed past them, running to get outside. One of them brushed her, making her stagger to keep her balance.

"Where the hell is everybody going in such a hurry?" the general asked.

"You got to see this, General," a man said as he went past.

Suddenly Beck heard the general's phone beep.

"Excuse me," he said to Beck, took out the phone, and stepped to one side of the hallway out of the now streaming herd of people headed for the door.

In a daze she headed for the door with them, since it was easier to follow the crowd at this point than fight with the general. She wasn't going to let his words stop her from fighting for her career. She had found the landing sight, saved all their lives, hadn't she? She would get back into space and be damned what the general thought.

Nothing was over.

Outside, in the warm night air, the crowd of people had spread out over the sidewalks and lawns. All of them were staring upward at the sky.

Three steps out the door and Beck could see why. In all her years she had never seen anything like it. The sky was lit up in multicolored shimmering lights, waves rolling through the colors like someone was brushing curtains—the Aurora Borealis in all its majestic beauty.

Vivid reds, blues, oranges, greens, made up a show that made her smile, even with the bad forecast the general had just given her. She had seen the northern lights before, but never this far south.

And never this bright.

It took a few more minutes of watching before she realized that such beauty in the sky was not necessarily a good thing. Something was causing this kind of odd occurrence.

Maybe it was the same something that caused the shuttle to crash? She had had enough basic physics to know it might be possible.

She turned and pushed her way through the sky-watching crowds. She had a few scientist friends who just might be able to answer that question for her. And maybe save her career.

Zimsky stared at the door through which Dr. Keyes had just left. Then he looked down at the papers on his desk. What Keyes had brought him wasn't possible, yet the calculations were spot on the money, the conclusions perfect.

Zimsky moved across his office to a place in front of what looked like a blank wall. He tapped a small area with his right finger. A laser took his fingerprint and the panel slid back. Inside the hidden security compartment were a number of files and computer disks, all detailing out a project code-named "Destiny."

Somehow his biggest fear was that Destiny had caused the problem Keyes had just discovered. He didn't how that could be, but anything was possible, and he had to make sure.

Zimsky opened one file and started to read. After a few minutes he opened another, then another, reviewing their contents, even though he knew it all very well.

It wasn't possible, yet the conclusion seemed impossible to ignore.

He put the files back into the cabinet, closed it, and moved over to his desk. His hands were shaking, his legs weak.

He lit a cigarette, moving as if sleepwalking, not wanting to sit down, not really wanting to think about the true meaning of what might happen. Between Dr. Keyes's calculations and the files in the safe, it was very possible Project Destiny had caused the problem. It was possible he had a hand in causing the destruction of all mankind.

He shook that thought away. Keyes's calculations

could not be right. But as he had said far too many times, math didn't lie. It misled at times, but it didn't lie. Let's hope right now it was just misleading, he thought.

Zimsky picked up his phone and dialed a number very few people on the planet knew. It was the personal line to General Thomas Purcell, one of the most powerful men in all the Pentagon. The man behind all the funding of Destiny.

The phone rang twice, then Purcell answered.

"Yes."

"Thomas," Zimsky said, "It seems that destiny may have caught up with us."

chapter four

THE BAR HAD A CLOUD OF SMOKE THAT SEEMED TO HANG HEAD-high all the way through the place, a blue-gray cloud that dimmed the few lights and made everything seem even fuzzier than the alcohol Josh had consumed.

By all standard terms that Josh knew, the bar was a dive, a place where only the locals went after work and where fights broke out in the parking lot on the weekends. It was a place that ignored the public area anti-smoking ordinances by simply not caring. Everything smelled of stale beer and unemptied ashtrays, and Josh had no doubt his clothes were going to stink when he got home, if he ever went home.

The bartender was a guy in his late fifties who wore an apron that had once been white and now looked crusty. He talked in short grunts, but charged decent prices for the beer.

This was Serge's favorite place, and Josh didn't care how much of a dive it was, as long as the guy behind the bar had enough bottles of beer for him, and wine for Serge.

The two of them had made camp in the corner booth, doing their best to not let themselves slide off the vinyl seats until they were too drunk to climb back on. Josh had managed six beers so far, and considering how rarely he drank, he was gaining on the sliding-off goal.

"*Merde, alors,*" Serge said, tipping up a small bottle of wine and finishing it off.

"Yep," Josh said, toasting his old friend with the remains in the bottle of beer. "Whatever."

Josh finished off the brew and banged the bottle on the table, pushing it to the center with the rest of the mess. If he wanted another one he was going to have to stagger to the bar. This place hadn't had a cocktail waitress in recent memory, and Josh doubted the bartender ever left the safety of the area behind the bar.

"Zimsky really tried to give you his autograph?" Serge asked, giggling.

When Josh had told him that earlier they had howled. Now Zimsky being an ass was the standing joke of the night that just seemed to get funnier and funnier with every beer.

Josh rubbed his eyes, noticing that his normal hangover was already starting with the throbbing in the back of his head.

"Oh, this is just great," Josh said. "I skipped over drunk and moved right to the hangover."

"Drink more," Serge said, laughing. "Go right from hangover to stupor."

Josh nodded. "Good idea. Anything to forget."

Serge got serious. "Any chance you're wrong?"

Josh pointed to the dark, smoke-stained ceiling over their heads. "That sky, man," he said, meaning the northern lights display they had both watched on the way into the bar. "That sky. It's the beginning."

"Why?" Serge asked.

"High altitude static discharge," Josh said.

"Oh," Serge said, shaking his head. "I hate it when that happens."

Josh laughed, then looked up as two guys in suits stopped in front of him. They towered over the table like giants. More FBI guys. Just great. Guys in suits was all he needed now.

He tried to peer up into the smoke to see if he knew them, but since they all looked the same, and he was drunk, he couldn't tell if they were the same two that had picked him up in Chicago, what now seemed like a lifetime ago.

"Dr. Keyes," one of the agents said, "your presence is required at the Pentagon."

"Oh, oh," Serge said. "Now you've done it."

"How did you find me?" Josh asked. He didn't much like the idea he was so damned easy to find anytime anyone snapped their political fingers.

"Join us for a drink first," Josh said, pointing at the open area of the booth.

"We'd be grateful," the man said, not even breaking a smile, "if you'd join us for a ride, sir."

Josh puffed himself up on the slick vinyl seat. "And if I say no?"

"We have no sense of humor," the agent said. "And we're armed."

Josh tossed Serge a large bill out of his wallet and stood, now sorry that he had had that last beer.

The hangover was clearly coming.

After fifteen minutes of driving with the window open, and two quick cups of coffee, Josh felt worse. The two agents escorted Josh into a large meeting room buried somewhere in the bowels of the Pentagon. Josh had no doubt he was still drunk, and smelled of smoke and beer. But since the world was coming to an end shortly, what difference did it make anyway?

The room was large, and there had to be at least twenty, maybe twenty-five people in it. Some of them wore uniforms with stars on them, others were scientists Josh either knew or recognized. It was an amazing gathering of power and brains. Josh just wished he was sober enough to enjoy it.

Off to one side, acting the fool as always, was Zimsky. Beyond him, at the front of the big conference table, someone had set up charts showing cross sections of the Earth. Uh-oh, clearly Zimsky had blabbed.

"Dr. Keyes," a voice said behind him.

Most of the talking in the room suddenly stopped as everyone turned to stare at him. Josh wanted to check to see if his fly was open, one of those automatic reactions after having too much to drink.

Josh turned slowly to see General Purcell smiling at him.

"Dr. Zimsky informs us that you made a useful contribution to his investigations. He wanted you to assist him with the briefing."

"That's very generous of you, Dr. Zimsky," Josh said. He knew this would happen. Although Josh had done the work, Zimsky was taking the credit.

Zimsky shrugged. "Science is a selfless business, dear boy. So why don't you begin and I'll fill in the difficult bits."

Josh just shook his head as a few people covered laughs. If he hadn't been so drunk, and if it had mattered any more, he might have been mad. As it was, it was stupid. It was amazing how knowing the world was going to end soon put a whole new perspective on things.

"All right," Josh said, moving to the front of the table, "I'm just drunk enough for this."

He stopped and looked at the generals and scientists, took a deep breath, and then said, "Everybody on Earth is dead in a year."

He knew he could have said that a little better, but what the hell. It got their attention.

A chorus of nervous chatter erupted.

Josh rubbed his eye, pushing back the hangover, and giving himself a moment to clear his mind and to let the weight of his words sink in. The room once again grew quiet when he continued to speak.

"Here's why," he said. He had their attention better than any class he had ever taught. "Wrapped around Earth is an invisible field of energy. It's made up of electricity and magnetism, so it's called, creatively enough, the Electromagnetic Field."

Almost everyone in the room nodded. So far they were with him.

"That field is where our north and south poles come from. It protects us from cosmic radiation. The EM Field is our friend."

"Now this field is falling apart," Zimsky said.

"Why?" someone with four stars on his shoulder asked from down the table.

"Could someone get me a can of air freshener?" Josh asked, going to a table set up with food. "And I'll show you."

A flunky, with a nod from General Purcell, left the room quickly.

Josh grabbed a peach, took a knife from a nearby serving area, and quickly cut the peach in half. Then he put the half with the pit still in it on a fork and held it up.

"Okay, quick and dirty," Josh said. "The thin skin. That's the Earth's Crust."

Josh pointed at the skin of the peach. "That's what we live on. It's thirty miles thick."

He pointed to the meat of the peach. "This area inside the Earth is called the Mantle. That makes up most of the Earth. Forgetting all the funky transitions, it's one thousand, eight hundred miles thick."

He glanced around. Everyone still seemed to be with him. "The Core—the peach pit, in the center—that's the tricky one, because there's two parts, the Inner and Outer Core. Following me?"

Most nodded.

"As the names would imply, the Inner Core is surrounded by the Outer Core, which is liquid."

"And most importantly," Zimsky chimed in, "that liquid is constantly spinning in one direction, a trillion, trillion tons of hot metal, spinning at a thousand miles an hour."

59

Josh smiled at all the scientists and generals. "Physics 101. Hot metal, moving fast, makes an electromagnetic field. The spinning Outer Core is the engine that drives the EM Field. And here's where we have our problem."

"The engine is stalled," Zimsky said. "The Core of the earth has stopped spinning."

Josh couldn't have said it better himself. He stood there as the group of scientists and generals soaked in that information, clearly shocked just trying to imagine it. Josh knew the feeling. He had had time trying to digest this one, and it wasn't going down easily.

"And how could this have happened?" General Purcell asked, staring at Zimsky.

Zimsky just stood there, not moving, or even making a motion to answer.

Josh noted the strange interchange, then decided to answer the general's question.

"We don't know. We do know that every seven-hundred-thousand years, or so, the Core changes direction. No big deal, since we've survived that many times."

The looks were blank.

Zimsky went on with the bad news. "But this time, with the Core stalled, the EM Field is falling apart."

"So now you get all this high weirdness," Josh said, playing tag with Zimsky in pounding these poor generals and scientists with too much information. "We've got electromagnetic pulses that fry pacemakers, overload bird navigational senses. More than likely messed up the Shuttle's navigation systems and caused that light show earlier this evening."

At that last comment General Purcell actually flinched for some reason Josh had no idea about. Then the general took a deep breath and asked, "What's the timeline here?"

Josh had had no doubt that question would come quickly. And since over the last few days he had worked out the answer, he knew it far better than he wanted to know. "As the EM Field becomes more and more unstable, we'll see isolated incidents. One airplane will fall from the sky, then two. In a few months everything electronic will be fried."

That caused an explosion of talking. These people all understood electronics, and how everything in modern civilization was tied to electronics, from phones to cars to computers.

General Purcell banged the table for quiet and motioned for Josh and Zimsky to go on.

Zimsky took the next batch of problems they would face. "Static discharge in the atmosphere will create 'super-storms' with hundreds of lightning strikes per square mile."

"And after that," Josh said, "well, then . . ." he

stopped and took a deep breath before being able to describe what would happen next. "Then it gets bad."

"The Earth's EM Field shields us from solar radiation," Zimsky said. "When that shield collapses, microwave radiation will scour the planet."

Josh noticed that the flunky had returned with the air freshener he had asked for. He moved over and took it, then spiked the half peach on a salad server and held it up.

"The sun," he said, holding up the air freshener can.

"Earth without an EM Field," he said, extending the peach stuck on the salad server.

"Would you?" Josh asked Zimsky.

Zimsky nodded, understanding what Josh was doing. He produced a lighter, and at the same moment that Josh started to spray the peach with the air freshener, Zimsky lit the spray.

The peach under the blow-torch effect of the burning spray, sputtered and quickly became a blackened coal. Josh had done this demonstration a dozen times in his class room, and it always got the same effect. Stunned silence.

Josh dropped the can and the sizzling peach onto the table.

"Four months, gentlemen," Zimsky said, "until we're back in the stone age. A full year, the EM Field collapses, and we end up like that."

He pointed at the burnt peach.

"Feel free to throw up," Josh said to the stunned faces in front of him. "I know I did."

At that moment Josh bet he could have heard a pin drop on the other side of the Pentagon. He knew how they were feeling. They had just been told the world was going to end, and that they were going to die a horrible, ugly death. Everyone was. There was no way to feel but stunned.

And hungover. He either needed aspirin, or some more beer. He didn't care which, actually.

"So, how do we fix it?" General Purcell asked.

Josh looked at him, shocked that the man could even ask such a stupid question. "We can't,"

"Not in my vocabulary," the general said.

"Then it's time to get one of those Word-A-Day calendars, General," Josh said, "Because it's impossible."

The general was about to object again, so Josh went on, trying not to show his frustration with the incredibly powerful and bright man.

"The Core of this planet is the size of Mars, general," Josh said, his words as level as he could make them. "You're talking about jump-starting a planet. It's superheated hyperfluid of molten nickel and iron at nine thousand degrees Fahrenheit. It's eighteen hundred miles down and a thousand miles thick. The deepest we've ever gone is seven miles, with a two inch drill bit."

"If we can go into space," the general said, "we can—"

"Space is easy!" Josh shouted at the man, finally not caring anymore that the guy could have him shot. "Space is empty! We're talking millions of pounds of pressure per square inch. Even if we somehow came up with a brilliant plan to fix the Core, we just can't get there."

The silence in the room was like a weight pressing all the air out of the place. More than anything else Josh just wanted to turn and leave, but since he was in the middle of the Pentagon, that wasn't going to be easy.

Then the silence was broken by Zimsky, asking him a question in a very small voice. "What if we could?"

"Could what?" Josh demanded, turning on the famous scientist.

"What if we could get there?" Zimsky asked, smiling.

Coming from anyone else, Josh would have laughed.

chapter five

JOSH HAD NO IDEA WHERE THEY WERE HEADING, OR EVEN WHY.
General Purcell and Dr. Zimsky would say nothing,
other than it was better that he wait and see when he
got there.

Serge completed the team. They had dragged him out
of bed, poured the hung-over man onto the airplane,
and let him sleep all the way to Salt Lake. Josh had done
his share of sleeping on the plane as well, and by the
time they arrived in Salt Lake, his hangover was gone,
and his appetite back. He managed to grab and down a
few large Danishes before they got off the plane.

He was still skeptical at the idea that there was anything man could do that would change what was coming. But at least trying to do something was better than
drinking and feeling sorry for himself.

In Salt Lake they were picked up by a military helicopter as they got off the private plane. Ten minutes after landing, they were back in the air and headed slightly south and west at top speed. Again, no one would tell him or Serge where they were going.

Then General Purcell pointed over a rise and Josh saw their destination ahead. From the air it looked like an abandoned military base, with a couple old hangars that hadn't been painted for decades, three smaller buildings, blowing sage brush, and rusting piles of junk that had been vehicles at one time. All around it was rock hills and salt flats. If there was a definition in the dictionary of "the middle of nowhere" this would be the picture.

The chopper did a quick turn and landed hard in front of the largest hangar, bouncing Josh in his seat. The dust the chopper blades kicked up hid everything for a moment. All of them stayed seated as the pilot cut the engine and waited for the dust to blow off to one side.

"Not good on a hangover," Serge said, holding his head.

"How long were you in that bar?" Josh asked the clearly pained Frenchman.

"It was a beautiful sunrise," Serge said.

General Purcell laughed.

That was all the information Josh needed. He patted

his friend's arm in sympathy as two soldiers riding behind them opened the door to the chopper and got out.

The hot air hit Josh like a slap, making him suddenly wish he hadn't choked down those two Danishes. The place had a salt smell, and felt extremely dry. Of course, considering that he was used to the humidity in Chicago and Washington, D.C., a shower often felt dry.

Zimsky climbed out of the helicopter right ahead of Josh and stepped to one side to light a smoke. Around them the silence had come in hard as the engine sounds died off. This was about as desolate and remote a place that Josh had ever been to.

"My lips just chapped," Serge said. "Where are we?"

No one answered Serge's question.

The four soldiers the general had brought along spread out, taking up positions around the helicopter, leaving the four of them standing on the dry, desert dirt.

Around them the old military base was even in worse condition than it had looked from the air. Tumbleweeds had filled up gaps along one wall of an old hangar, and the faint signs of letters were still visible over one big door. Josh couldn't make out what they used to say.

He was about to ask what was next when a hangar door started to slide open, sending screeching noises echoing against the rock face and salt flats beyond the old buildings.

A man in his late forties stepped from the hangar and walked toward the group, not seeming at all surprised that there was a military helicopter parked there. He looked like a mountain man and wore a stained shirt and khaki pants.

"Hello, Brazzle," Zimsky said.

Josh glanced at Zimsky, then at the man headed their way. Could this guy actually be the famous Dr. Ed Brazzleton, the most reclusive and brilliant of working scientists in the country? Everyone had heard of Brazzleton. No one Josh knew had ever met him.

Brazzleton stopped a short distance away, staring at Zimsky. "Why aren't you dead yet?"

Then Brazzleton turned and walked away, heading for a building tucked against a rock ledge.

Zimsky glanced over at the smiling face of General Purcell. "That went better than I expected."

General Purcell just shook his head and started out after Brazzleton, the others following behind almost running to catch up. They finally joined him, maintaining the scientist's steady pace.

"You've been smoking since college," Brazzleton said to Zimsky without really looking at him. "Millions of good people die every year from smoking. I've seen the ads."

Zimsky glanced at Purcell, then at Josh. "He still holds a grudge. I can't believe this."

Josh said nothing. Considering his short time in working with Zimsky, he could find it completely understandable why another scientist would hold a grudge.

"Dr. Brazzleton," the general said, still matching Brazzleton's stride through the heat toward a large building ahead of them. "I'm General Thomas Purcell, United States Army. Dr. Joshua Keyes and Dr. Serge Leveque are consulting for the government. I see you know Dr. Zimsky."

Brazzleton snorted. "Sort of. Twenty years ago he stole my research. Since then we've lost touch."

"Research that was equally mine," Zimsky said.

To Josh, that sounded very, very lame. And very familiar.

Again Brazzleton just snorted and kept walking. "I don't remember a check from any of those patents."

Zimsky waved away the words. "Yes, yes, twenty years in the desert makes you a prophet and a martyr. We're here about your legendary ship."

Now Josh was really confused. He had heard nothing about a ship that Dr. Brazzleton was working on. The man was famous for many things, including developments in lasers and metals, but never building ships of any type, as far as Josh knew.

"I didn't figure you'd come for the scenery," Brazzleton said. He stopped and faced General Purcell. "Is it really a matter of national security."

Purcell nodded.

Brazzleton shook his head and turned and headed for a rusted Jeep parked beside the large building. Clearly he expected them to follow and get in. Josh wasn't sure if he wanted to ride in anything that didn't have a top, and was built before the words "seat belts" had been thought of.

"What ship?" Josh whispered to Serge as they scrambled for the Jeep.

"A ship that bores through rock," Serge said.

Josh doubted it could bore through enough rock in the time they had left. But as long as he'd been dragged all the way to Utah, he figured he may as well take a ride.

General Purcell took the passenger seat, leaving Zimsky, Serge, and Josh the back area of the old Jeep. The seat was coated in a layer of sand and dirt, and it looked like an animal had built a nest under it, but Josh didn't have time to brush it off as Dr. Brazzleton fired up the old motor and jerked the Jeep into motion, not even checking to see if they were in.

All Josh could do was hold on as Brazzleton bounced them a quarter mile down a path that no one in the modern world would ever call a road.

Brazzleton stopped the Jeep in front of a granite rock face that towered over the desert floor by at least a hundred feet. At the base of the cliff Brazzleton had a couple of instruments, some covered, some sitting out in the sun and dust. Here, with the sun reflecting off the rock, as well as the sand, the temperature seemed even hotter. There was no doubt to Josh that he was going to need water and shade pretty soon.

Brazzleton headed for one instrument that looked like a long gun barrel set on a tripod and aimed at the rock face. It had wires running from the tripod to a computer monitor under a cover, and another larger wire running off through the sand.

"Power cable," Brazzleton said, indicating the cable that disappeared into the sand. "This is the basis of the boring mechanism for the ship. "I'm combining high-frequency, pulsed lasers with resonance tube ultrasonics."

Josh glanced at Serge, who was staring at the tube, nodding.

"Y'ever see ultrasonic waves break up a kidney stone on the Discovery Channel?" Brazzleton asked. "This is the same deal. The laser melts the rock, the ultrasonics break it up."

Brazzleton handed them all some bulky ear protection. Josh had barely had time to get it on his head and over his ears when Brazzleton fired his experiment.

A low, subsonic hum jarred Josh's teeth and mouth. Then the noise quickly escalated into a painful pounding that felt like waves hitting his head from both sides, banging at his ears. Josh didn't want to think what it sounded like without the ear protection.

Then Brazzleton hit a switch and a laser snapped out of the metal barrel at the rock face. A half second later it was gone, and so was the sound.

The relief of the silence was almost too much. It was as if the sound still echoed inside his head.

Josh let out the breath he had been holding and took off the ear protection. Sweat was running down his face, drying almost instantly.

Brazzleton walked up to the rock face where the laser had hit, with the rest of them following.

"How's that for you?" Brazzleton asked.

The hole in the rock was about the size of a thumb. Nothing impressive at all.

"It's seventy feet deep, you know," Brazzleton said.

Josh peered into the hole. The depth was something new, but not something that was going to save the planet in the next few months.

"Twenty years?" Zimsky said. "That's as far as you got?"

Brazzleton shook his head in disgust and strode toward a large, bulky object to one side, covered by a tarp.

"Actually," he said, more to himself than anyone else, "I got a little farther."

Brazzleton yanked off the tarp showing a large engine the size of a turbine. From what Josh could tell, the center was made up of at least fifty of the tubes, shaped in the form of a Gatling gun.

"Firing," Brazzleton said, putting on his headgear.

Josh barely got his back on in time as the monster engine started up.

The tubes in the center of the engine started to rotate, spinning up so fast that they disappeared into a giant blur.

The sound was like nothing Josh had ever experienced before. Every cell in his head felt like it would explode at any moment. He held his hands over the large ear protection, pushing inward, hoping it would help some.

It didn't.

Then suddenly a beam of heat and sonic and light snapped out from the huge engine and smashed into the cliff face. The impact knocked Josh and everyone but Brazzleton from their feet.

An instant later it was done.

Josh just lay there in the dirt, panting, as the cloud of dust swirled over him, slowly moving away in the slight breeze. His ears were ringing, his head was pounding, and he doubted he was ever going to get the dust and grime out of his mouth and eyes.

Beside him Serge, covered in white dust, looked like he might throw up at any moment.

The general and Zimsky slowly climbed to their feet to be met by the smiling Brazzleton, his face also coated in dust. Josh stood and helped Serge up. The pounding in his head was slowly subsiding, but he desperately needed some water.

"Well?" Brazzleton asked, pointing at the rock as the dust cleared.

Josh turned, and couldn't believe what he saw. A hole, seventy feet deep and the size of a subway tunnel, its edges perfectly smooth, fused together by the intense heat of the laser.

Josh slowly moved up to the hole, making sure to not touch anything, and peered inside. It went a good twenty-five or thirty paces into the rock.

"Okay," Josh said, turning to the stunned, dirt-covered faces of Zimsky, Serge, and General Purcell. "I'm officially impressed."

chapter six

JOSH THOUGHT HE WAS GOING TO DIE OF THIRST BY THE TIME they got back to Dr. Brazzleton's lab. The doctor took a towel and wiped off his own face, then tossed it to Josh and pointed to other towels and wash cloths hanging near a utility sink. Then Brazzleton went to a refrigerator filled with bottled water.

Josh washed off his face, and then finally let himself look around after he had downed a half bottle of the best tasting water he could remember. The lab was as dusty and chaotic as everything outside, with parts of machines everywhere, in seemingly no order. But some of the devices tucked in among the junk were top of the line instruments. Clearly Dr. Brazzleton had money.

"Okay," Zimsky said, "you've got an engine, but no

shell. Several million pounds of pressure per square inch, heat in the thousands of degrees—"

All Dr. Brazzleton did was half-chuckle. He first moved over to a cabinet, unlocked it, and pulled out a small, blue-black box. He carried it over to a center table and put it on a concrete block in front of a two-inch thick steel plate, square in the line of fire of a laser.

Brazzelton then motioned to an assistant, who brought over a cage with a small white mouse inside. He took out the mouse, put it in the box and closed the lid.

"Everyone knows boron nitride crystals are six times harder than diamonds." Dr. Brazzleton said, glancing around at his audience.

Even the general nodded on that one.

Brazzleton went on. "But nobody could figure out how to fabricate the crystals into something useful."

His audience stood transfixed.

Brazzleton moved over and started the laser. It hit the box with the mouse in it, engulfed it completely, then hit the steel plate behind it.

The steel plate melted like hot butter, then the concrete slab behind the steel plate started to melt as well.

Brazzleton turned off the laser just before all the concrete had been destroyed.

All Josh could do was stare. The blue-black box with

the mouse inside was untouched by a laser that melted steel and concrete.

Brazzleton put on two fireproof gloves that smoldered as they touched the box. Carefully he flipped open the lid. Then just as carefully, he lifted out an untouched mouse, still very much alive and well and unharmed in any fashion, and carried the creature back to its cage.

"That's impossible," both Serge and Josh said at exactly the same time.

Dr. Brazzleton only shrugged and motioned that they should look over his shoulder at a large computer screen. With a few quick keystrokes he displayed a mind-bogglingly complex molecule, like none other Josh had ever seen. None of the properties of the molecule even seemed to resemble anything Josh was used to working with.

"I discovered," Brazzleton said, "that combining the crystals in a tungsten-titanium matrix at supercool temperatures did the trick."

The general tried to explain what Brazzleton had told him previously. "The applications for this are—" but he couldn't find words for what he was thinking. Josh had no doubt the general had ideas for this new material that no one in the private sector even dreamed about. But considering the world was about to end, what did it matter?

"What do you call it?"

Brazzleton laughed. "It's real name has thirty-seven syllables," he said. "I call it Unobtainium."

Josh finished off his bottle of water. "I'd say you have at least three Nobel prizes coming to you for this. But we don't have a lot of time here, so . . . er . . . how's the ship itself coming?"

For the first time Josh was actually starting to think that someone had invented a ship that might dive down into the earth's crust, maybe even to the mantle. But unless this ship was sitting outside in one of those hangars, they, and all the world, were still screwed.

"Great," Brazzleton said, and started leading them all back out into the heat and sun.

They headed toward the hangar he had come from when they first landed. The soldiers were still at their posts, standing in the sun, protecting the helicopter. Josh wondered if any of them were allowed to drink, or were they just going to have to drop from sunstroke before someone thought to give them shade and a bottle of water.

"Unobtainium takes heat and pressure," Brazzleton said as they walked across the open area, "and transforms them into energy. The deeper and hotter she goes, the stronger she gets. Theoretically."

So they really were talking about a ship that could dive into the rock and go deep.

"Theoretically." Zimsky asked.

"What is the maximum temperature it could handle?" Serge asked.

"Nine thousand degrees Fahrenheit," Brazzleton said. Then added, "Theoretically."

"Temperature of the Core," Josh said. "Think she can take that?"

Brazzleton snorted as he opened the hangar door, rolling it back on its rusted wheels. "Oh, she'll take the heat, boy. She'll take it."

Josh wasn't sure what he expected to find inside that hangar, but it sure wasn't what he saw there. The place was littered with odd engine and car-body parts, most of them in piles and various forms of disassembly. All of it was covered with a pretty thick layer of dust, as if nothing had been touched in years. There was even a few old truck bodies sitting to one side.

But there was no rock-diving ship.

The hangar instead looked more like a scene from a junkyard than a place where any kind of high-tech ship was being built.

"Dr. Brazzleton," General Purcell said, shocked at what he saw. Or more likely, at the lack of what he saw, "When do you think this ship could be operational?"

Brazzleton walked a few steps into the hangar, then turned around, smiling. "Made a lot of progress lately.

Once some of our fabrication methods are perfected, twelve, maybe ten years."

Josh managed to not laugh. There wasn't anything funny about what the man had just said. He had just doomed them again.

The general looked Dr. Brazzleton right in the eye. "What would it take to get it done in three months?"

Dr. Brazzleton stared at the general for a moment, then started laughing, as if he were watching the funniest movie in the world. None of the rest of them laughed.

It felt odd to Josh to just stand there and watch a man laugh. Under normal circumstances, it might be funny in and of itself, but at the moment Josh was not finding one lousy thing funny about it.

Finally Brazzleton managed to calm down a little. He took a deep breath, and still containing his laughter said, "Got a billion dollars?"

The general didn't flinch.

None of the rest of them even cracked a smile.

The general, serious as a heart attack, continued to stare directly at Brazzleton. "Will you take a check?"

"Use a credit card. You get the miles," Josh suggested dryly.

The knock at the door sounded like a death toll to Theodore Donald Finch, aka Rat. No one knew he was here, and he hadn't ordered pizza or Chinese. Besides, he knew that type of knock anywhere. That knock had come twice before, on his two previous arrests, so he wasn't completely surprised when it was followed by "FBI. Open up!"

"Shit!" Rat said, looking around at his apartment. The entire room was crammed with wall-to-wall computers and electronic equipment. It was the most sophisticated setup he'd ever had. Now it was lost. Multiple screens, the best in power supplies, everything, all wasted.

"Shit! Shit! Shit!"

He had no way out. None. The best he could do was cover what he'd been up to and hope the judge went light on him.

Bang! Bang! Bang!

"Open up!"

Shit! They weren't fooling around. They were coming in and there was nothing he was going to do to stop them.

He dropped into one chair and his fingers flew over the keyboard. Suddenly all the screens in the room scrambled and were replaced with the words "Core purge."

He grabbed a stack of floppy disks, jumped up, and shoved them down the dirty sink's garbage disposal. Then he turned it on. It would take a better hacker than he was to get any information off of those after that.

The sound was like a monster had entered the room as the disposal worked to chew up the metal and plastic of the disks. And it made the guys outside the door angry, for some reason. They started working to break in the door. Luckily he had invested in a pretty good reinforcing bar to put across it. They were going to get in, but it was going to take them a minute.

He took his only stack of CDs and tossed them into the microwave, then turned it on.

Sparks flew from both the microwave and the CDs inside. Nothing would be salvageable from those either.

Now he just had to get rid of the ghosts on his drives.

He grabbed two large electromagnets he had bought just for this emergency. He plugged them in and started passing them over each hard drive, making sure that nothing was left on any of the systems. He was almost done, just one hard drive away from taking care of any evidence that he was actually hacking systems, when the door slammed open and an agent in a black suit shouted, "Freeze!"

He stood there, staring down the barrels of five pistols and one shotgun.

"Okay," he said, nodding to all the equipment. "You

probably think these are computers." He shook his head. "Totally not."

From the looks on the cold faces of the men facing him, they didn't believe him.

He lowered the magnets slowly and sat them on the last hard drive he needed to erase, then with a smile he slowly raised his hands.

chapter seven

Josh stood in the fortieth floor office suite that General Purcell said was rented by the government. It looked more like the executive offices of a Fortune 500 company than a government office. A lot more, especially considering the leather furniture, oak tables, and marble bathroom fixtures.

Both Josh and Serge had helped themselves to the food supplied on a side table, and were now standing at the window looking out at the view of New York City. The last few days had been something Josh would not soon forget, yet at the same time the days and the events didn't seem real.

Discovering that the world was about to end was enough, but then finding out there actually was a slim chance they could stop this was something else again.

He still didn't believe it, didn't believe Dr. Brazzleton's discoveries, even though he had seen them with his own eyes.

But having something work in a test, and building something that would work on a major scale, in the most trying of field conditions, were two different things. And he certainly doubted that they could start the entire center of the planet spinning again, if they could get there.

Especially when there was no time to spare at all.

Which was why they were here, today, in New York. They were trying to buy civilization a little time. They were about to set about on one of the largest cover-ups in all time. It would be so wide-ranging that it would make Watergate look like a child's game.

And Josh completely agreed it had to be done one moment, and hated the thought of doing it the next. Part of him thought that people should be allowed to know their life was about to end. And then he knew what that knowledge would mean on a mass scale, including riots, murders, and all the awful things about man that the surface of civilization barely kept under control.

He and those who knew what was coming had to have time to at least try to fix it, no matter how remote the chance of success. And the only way to do that was to lie to the entire planet.

Zimsky sat at a table, smoking, while General Purcell waited, standing easily by the door. None of them were talking. After the last few days, there just wasn't much they could talk about.

Josh had returned to the food table when there was a single knock and the door opened.

Josh turned to face the two agents escorting a young, scrawny kid into the room. The kid had spiked hair, dirty, patched jeans, and a tee shirt that looked stained by a dozen meals.

"Is this the best we could come up with?" Zimsky asked, clearly disgusted at the sight of the small, skinny kid.

Josh, on the other hand, had worked with young students over the last few years at the university. He was a long way from judging this book by its cover. It was often the smartest kids who had the most problems with simple things like taking a shower every day.

The two agents left the kid and closed the door behind them on the way out.

"Theodore Donald Finch," General Purcell said. "Carnegie-Mellon University, M.I.T., worked at Sun, Lucent, and Rand Corp."

"This is new," the kid said, glancing around at the plush suite. "And it's Rat. My handle's Rat."

"Sixty-three computer fraud indictments," General Purcell went on, as if reading the kids life story. "Two convictions. This is strike three, Mr. Finch. You were supposed to stay away from computers as a condition of your parole."

Rat glanced first at the general, then at Serge and Josh, who had moved closer to be in on the discussion. "Oh, man, you guys aren't gonna whack me, are you? I was really, really hoping to have sex before that happened."

Josh managed to keep a straight face, but Serge snorted his coffee.

General Purcell went on. "I was informed by the FBI, whose databases you crippled last year, that you're the best in the business. So you're about to be given a choice."

"What if I say no?" Rat asked, focusing on the general.

"Enjoy that view for one last time," Zimsky said, pointing at the window.

Josh stepped up to Rat, figuring it was time to play a little good cop here to the general's bad cop. "Look, Rat, we have a big problem. A lot of people are going to die. We need your help."

Rat sort of stood up straighter, then glanced at the general, who nodded.

"What kind of help?" Rat asked. He reached out and took Josh's cell phone from his breast pocket, faster than Josh could even move to stop him. Then using the quickest, wiriest fingers Josh had ever seen, Rat started fiddling with the cell phone as if he were simply doodling.

"You'll be briefed in full detail if you accept the assignment," the general said. "But let me say that your primary assignment and responsibility is information control."

Rat shrugged, still working on the phone. "There's other guys who can do that. Networking stuff."

Rat took out a pack of Juicy Fruit gum, took out a piece, tossed the gum onto the table, and started folding the tin foil, holding Josh's cell phone under his arm. Josh desperately wanted to grab the phone back, yet at the same time was fascinated that someone could hold a conversation and fiddle with a phone like Rat was doing. Finally, Josh forced himself back to the conversation. "Not on a network. On the Internet. We need you to control the flow of information on the Net."

Josh didn't want to tell Rat at this point the importance of the task they were asking him to do. The news about the coming disaster had to be stopped at all costs, in a thousand different places, and the worst place, and the hardest to control, was on the Internet.

"You're dreaming," Rat said, taking the folded tin foil and putting it between the teeth of an old black comb. "Nobody controls the Net."

He blew across the foil and the comb, making a high-pitched whine.

"Could you do it with unlimited resources?" Josh asked.

"You want me to hack the Net?" Rat asked, staring at him.

"Yes," Josh said.

Rat took Josh's cell phone and blew across the comb into it. A moment later there was a sudden modem static sound. Rat nodded, punched in a number, waited a few moments for a few beeps that Josh could hear, then smiled and tossed Josh the phone. "You've got free long distance on that phone. Forever."

Then he turned to the general. "I'll do it, but I'll need *Xena* tapes and Hot Pockets. They help me concentrate."

All of them nodded, as if that request was just something standard. Josh just stared at his cell phone, wondering what he was going to do with it now.

Beck sat on the bench outside the courtroom, chewing gum like it was her last meal. The moment the flavor of one stick was gone, she tossed it into the ashtray beside the bench and got another. She had already gone through two packs and was starting on the third.

The hallway had been crowded at times, then not crowded. She had no idea how long she had been sitting out here in her dress uniform, waiting for her chance to testify in the official accident investigation, but she expected to sit most of the afternoon, just waiting.

Suddenly a court officer stuck his head out of the door and motioned for her to come inside.

Too soon. That was too fast. Commander Iverson should still be working over the details of what had happened. This could only mean that they had already all made up their minds.

She took the gum out of her mouth, straightened her dress uniform, and went into full military mode. If nothing else, she was going to act the part of an officer, even if they were about to take her career away from her.

Two air force officers she did not recognize sat behind a large table at the end of the room. Both were generals, both had three stars. That was about what she would expect to be on a panel investigating something as important as the crash of a shuttle.

To their right were three NASA officials. Beck knew all three of them by name, but nothing more. None of them looked friendly at the moment.

Sitting in front of the panel was Commander Iverson. He glanced around at her. From the look on his face, he was not happy with the way things were going, either. Not happy at all.

Sitting to the right of Iverson was Stickley. She also was not smiling.

"Major Rebecca Childs, reporting, General," she said, snapping to attention beside Iverson and then saluting the man in the center of the table.

"Major Childs," the general said, returning the salute and then glancing at his notes. "At ease."

She dropped to parade rest position, staring straight ahead as she had been trained.

"A clarification, please," the general said, looking up at her. "You, and you alone, were responsible for proposing the descent vectors for the shuttle, correct?"

"Sir, permission to speak?" she said.

"Yes or no will do, Major," the general said.

"Yes, General," she said.

She desperately wanted to scream at them, to fight back with all her will, but her training kept her in check, kept her standing there, eyes forward, as they flushed her career down the toilet.

The general nodded, then with a glance at the other members of the panel, he looked up at her. "We have determined that the Class A landing mishap experienced by the shuttle *Endeavor*, was caused by biased navigational data from the ground due to a brief geomagnetic disturbance."

She just stared at him, not really understanding where he was heading. If the problem hadn't been hers, or anyone else's on the shuttle, how could they drop her from the program? Yet they had just stated, on the record, that the problem had been a fluke, and had come from the ground control.

"Major Childs," the general went on, "the resourcefulness you showed in determining the descent vectors proved that you have exceptional navigational skills. You have brought great credit upon yourself, the space program, and the United States Air Force. Congratulations, Major."

Beck stood there, stunned, not knowing what to say. Never had the tables been so turned on her, so completely and fully. The world around her was spinning. She forced herself to take a deep breath. Her career was still intact.

But it seemed the general wasn't done yet.

"Major, you are reassigned with Commander Iverson and Flight Director Stickley to a new mission. Effective immediately. Transportation is waiting outside. Good luck, and Godspeed, Major."

The panel stood and turned to leave as Beck stared at their backs, then at the stunned faces of Commander Iverson and Stickley.

"What just happened here?" she asked.

The commander only shrugged.

"I have no idea," Stick said, shaking her head. "But I have a sneaking suspicion we're going to find out shortly."

Beck managed another breath, then turned and followed Commander Iverson from the room. Of all the outcomes she might have guessed, a commendation and immediate reassignment was not among them.

Had the world just tipped on its head? Or were the northern lights getting to people? Because none of this made any sense.

chapter eight

JOSH PACED THE FAIRLY SMALL ROOM OFF TO THE SOUTH SIDE OF what was quickly becoming Mission Control. Over the last few days he had been constantly astounded at how fast things were moving. After the meeting in New York, he and Serge had gone back to Dr. Brazzleton's base in the Utah desert. When they arrived they almost didn't recognize the place.

A massive runway had already been built on the salt flat, long enough to easily handle their private jet. When they stepped out into the heat of the late afternoon, three cargo planes were unloading what looked like enough materials to build an entire town.

Two large dorm structures had been built in the two days they had been gone, just to the west of the original hangar building. It had, from what Josh had been told, one of the most extensive kitchens ever designed and built in a day. It could feed up to a thousand, and General Purcell noted later that there would be a second, bigger kitchen built in a week in a mess building.

Another housing building for Josh and some of the top brass, including Serge and Zimsky, had been built right near the house Brazz had lived in for years. It had two-room suites and just about everything a man could ask for, including a large television and a small kitchen of its own.

The old main hangar, that a few days ago held only dust-covered parts, now looked like the center of a vast construction project, with scaffolding already up around what would become their ship, and two dozen men quickly putting on a new roof and extending the back wall by four hundred feet to allow for manufacturing areas.

Josh had been told that there were at least three hundred soldiers working in the desert around the base, building a huge fence and pounding large Classified Area: Use of Deadly Force Authorized signs everywhere. Fighter jets were already starting to patrol the area twenty-four hours a day.

General Purcell was taking no chances. Josh liked that.

A number of smaller jets, clearly chartered, with scientists from all over the world, were also starting to arrive. An hour after each arrival, a new flag would be erected on a new flagpole in the main area outside the hangar.

The place was starting to look like the United Nations. By the end of the third day there were over thirty countries represented in the Utah desert, the best gathering of minds Josh could have ever imagined. He had seen the list, and it had shocked him.

And now, this evening, they were all coming together in one large area, taking chairs in rows facing a stage. None of them really knew exactly why they were here. Only that it was of extreme importance, and about world security.

But shortly everyone would know.

General Purcell had chosen Josh to tell them. And to lead the entire mission.

Why he had been picked, he had no idea, but it was the reason he was pacing in the small room off the large hangar, and working to knot his tie. He had never had trouble knotting a tie before. Never. This did not bode well for the coming speech.

"How are you holding up?" the general asked.

Josh shrugged and again started on the tie. "I'm about to tell a couple of hundred people that it's the end of the world. I've had better days."

Zimsky moved over and stood next to the general, ignoring Josh. "Thomas, wouldn't you rather I did this? I think my reputation would make—"

"I want Keyes in the lead here, Zimsky."

Josh glanced at Zimsky, who just glared and shook his head. Clearly he wasn't used to playing second fiddle to anyone.

"This is the most important scientific operation in history. I think it's my job—"

The general cut him off with a wave of his hand. "Project Destiny was your job, Zimsky. And you went way beyond authorized limits." The general stopped and stared at the short scientist. "I still want to know, did Destiny cause this problem?"

"Highly unlikely," Zimsky said. "But it still could be the solution. I'm still studying the data from the test firings."

The general waved off the man's answer and turned to the door as two people entered the room.

Josh desperately wanted to ask the general exactly what this Destiny project was. But he knew better.

From the way Zimsky was acting about it, there was no getting the information from him, either. But it must have been something important, and concerning deep-Earth research, if the general was that angry about it.

Josh ignored Zimsky as the general greeted a man in his early forties, and a woman who looked like she should be on a runway modeling high fashion.

Josh felt his stomach flip just looking at her. He knew that face, had seen it on magazines over the years. That was Major Childs, the astronaut who had figured out how to keep the shuttle from plowing a path of destruction through Los Angeles. Not only was she an astronaut, she was brilliant *and* beautiful.

The general shook their hands, and said something to them that Josh couldn't hear. Then the general turned to the rest of the room and said loud enough for everyone to hear, "Commander Iverson, Colonel Childs, meet your crew."

It was clear to Josh that Commander Iverson didn't much like what he saw, even though the commander tried to smile. And Josh didn't really blame him.

Colonel Childs, on the other hand, smiled in such a way that Josh almost melted and screwed up his tie again.

The general continued the introductions as people shook hands.

"Dr. Brazzleton knows the ship. Dr. Zimsky knows the planet. Dr. Leveque knows the weapons systems, Dr. Keyes built your navigation system and is supervising the project. These are your fellow—"

The general paused, not knowing what exactly to call the crew.

"Terranauts?" Beck said, as she shook Josh's hand and looked at him like no one had looked at him before.

Josh liked her grip. Firm and solid, yet still a woman's grip.

And he *loved* her eyes. Their gazes held for a moment before she let go of his hand.

At that moment Josh decided that if the world was going to end, spending the last days with Beck Childs might not be such a bad way of going out.

At that moment Stickley punched her head in the door. "All that brainpower out there's starting to smell like burning batteries. You better come and get this started."

The general nodded and lead Brazzleton and Zimsky out the door behind Stickley.

Josh sighed. "Well, it's official. I am the least qualified person on this base."

Commander Iverson had the decency to laugh lightly. "Dr. Keyes, I'm sure the people in charge have full confidence in you."

"The problem is—" Josh said, still trying to get his tie done correctly. "I'm in charge."

Stickley, commanded everyone's attention and started making introductions out in the main hangar. Iverson turned and headed in that direction as Beck stepped toward Josh. "Can I help you with that?"

Her voice could melt butter as far as Josh was concerned. And the slight smile on her face froze him in his tracks.

Without waiting for a reply, she took his tie, yanked it free, and started working on it again, her hands moving as if she had done this a thousand times.

"You're an astronaut, and you can tie a full Windsor," Josh said, her face very close to his, her wonderful fresh smell covering him. "Is there anything you can't do?"

"Not that I'm aware of," she said, smiling up at him, then going back to work on the tie.

"I find that incredibly intimidating," Josh said.

"Most people do," Beck said, jerking the tie up against his neck.

With a glance into the mirror, and a nod of thanks to her, they headed into the large room just as Stickley introduced them. With his tie done right, and Colonel Childs at his side, he felt, for the first time today that he might get through this.

If getting through meant not feeling completely helpless telling the top minds in the world that they, and everyone they knew would all soon be dead without some sort of miracle here in the Utah desert.

Josh felt he was going to be lucky if he didn't get lynched.

After Dr. Keyes' talk, and the hundred questions that followed, Beck found herself out walking under the flags toward the airstrip, almost like a zombie in the warm, dry air.

They had been told on the way to Utah that she and Commander Iverson were to "pilot" a ship that dug into rock, crewed by a bunch of scientists, and that Stickley was to be flight controller.

That news had made them all angry. She was an astronaut, not a rock hound. She had figured that she would resign after a day or so, and go find something worth her time.

When she saw General Purcell, she knew right then that this was something more important than tossing the three of them aside and literally burying them.

Then Josh's talk had shocked her down to the base of her spine. It wasn't possible that the entire world was going to come to an end, yet above her, to the north, the first signs of northern lights for the evening were flickering in the sky. Something had to be causing such a change, to have caused the shuttle navigation system to dump them into Los Angeles.

All the facts were in front of her that something major was going wrong. She just didn't want to believe that the entire center of the Earth's core had stopped moving. And because of that, they were all going to die.

That was just not something that went down easily.

And the fact that she was going to try to change that didn't register at all with her. A planet was a big thing. You didn't just go spinning one at will.

She went out to a rock on the edge of the runway and sat down, watching as cargo plane after cargo plane landed and soldiers scrambled to unload them.

The way the planes were coming in here, this makeshift field was becoming one of the busiest airports in the country.

Dr. Keyes had said that utmost secrecy at all levels had to be maintained, and that a major thrust around the world was being put forth to keep this news completely secret until they had a chance to try to fix the problem. But Beck just couldn't believe that all of this activity could be kept quiet.

And how were the scientists around the world explaining all the strange things, like the northern lights? They didn't have enough time to build this ship, learn how to pilot it, and then go solve the problem. What they were trying to do was more ambitious than going to the moon, even to Mars, yet they were going to try to do it in less than three months.

Beck just shook her head at the idea.

After an hour or so, she finally decided that the only way she was ever going to really believe this was all happening was to go back and talk to people about it, get more information, make things concrete in her mind.

She headed for the big hangar first, figuring that if the ship was going to be built in there, that would be the best place to start.

A guard nodded to her and opened the door, letting her into the old building that was now flooded with bright lights, a new concrete floor, and a ton of equipment.

Dr. Brazzleton was walking a group of scientists and technicians along the scaffolding that was filling the center of the huge hangar, pointing at areas of the skeleton of the ship.

"The melted slag will be expelled by the impellers through these manifolds," Dr. Brazzleton said, pointing to an empty area as those around him nodded, clearly following him. "This gives us steering and propulsion."

Beck shook her head. Okay, she was going to pilot a ship that used melted slag as fuel as it bored through rock.

Dr. Brazzleton continued. "Top speed of sixty to seventy-five mph. Theoretically. Question is—how do we prevent this material from solidifying before two hundred feet of ship has passed through it."

Beck shook her head. That had been too much information for the night. She was going to be piloting a ship that used slag as propulsion, that was two hundred feet long, and went seventy miles per hour through solid rock.

None of this could be real.

She spun on her heel and left, heading back out into the warm night with the beautiful northern lights dancing in the sky overhead, covering her beloved stars.

She headed for the building where her room was. What she really needed was to curl up in bed, pull the covers over her head, and pretend that when she woke up in the morning, this would all be a bad dream.

And she did just that. But the next morning the world was still the same, and she had decided, at some point during the sleepless night, that if she was ever going to get back into space, she needed to get to the center of the Earth, and save it first.

At first light, as soon as the northern lights quit dancing in the sky, she headed to the kitchen for breakfast. She wasn't the first one there.

chapter nine

SOMEHOW, JOSH HAD MANAGED TO GET THREE HOURS OF SLEEP A night for the last five nights, as more and more people poured into the base, and more and more problems got solved almost as fast as they came up.

Everyone had their duties, and seemed to focus on their own area, leaving him time to work on the communications systems. General Purcell ran all the daily activity on the base, and a three-person delegation from the United Nations worked with the scientists from different countries, seeing to their needs.

He had also, somehow, managed to avoid spending too much time over the last few days with Colonel Childs. There was just something about that woman that attracted him, and scared him to death at the same time. And considering that the world was about to end, being scared seemed foolish at best. But he couldn't help it. And he didn't have time for it.

Considering that they were trying to do the impossible, and had just built a base the size of a decent town in seven days, Josh was encouraged.

However, this morning, nine short, but very intense days after first visiting Dr. Brazzleton, they were facing the biggest "what-if" they had yet to face, and as far as Josh as concerned, it wasn't going well.

"My calculations show," Zimsky said, pointing to a computer simulation of the Earth's core, "that a tiny nudge in any direction will force the core back into its normal flow."

Around the lab Serge, Commander Iverson, General Purcell, Beck, and Josh were listening to Zimsky talk. The morning was already turning hot outside, but at least the new air conditioners were working, keeping the rooms and labs fairly cool.

"What's a tiny nudge in planetary terms?" Josh asked, then took a drink from the half-finished bottle of water in his hand. Josh had made it a habit to have a water bottle in his hands from the moment he woke up to the moment he tried to sleep. He figured in this heat and dry climate, it was just safer that way.

"A thousand megatons, give or take?" Serge said.

"Tops," Zimsky said. "Any more could create a Core instability."

Josh agreed with the size of explosion, and was about to ask Zimsky what he considered a core instability, then decided not to. They were facing more than enough troubles as it was. No point in worrying about one more.

The room waited as Serge quickly did a search of the computer database on his laptop. After a moment he smiled and turned the screen around for the rest of them to see.

"Our atomic weapons program made a few monster warheads in the two hundred megaton range," he said. "Big is beautiful, no?"

On the screen Josh could see a schematic of a cluster of five, large nuclear weapons. If each was two hundred, that totaled a thousand right there.

"So," Josh said, shaking his head, "the world's biggest weapons of mass destruction are going to save the world. Irony actually breaks for the good guys for once."

Commander Iverson snorted. "I'm not the expert here, but what if the Core isn't what you think it is?"

Everyone looked at him as the silence in the lab grew.

Iverson went on. "What if it's thicker, or thinner? Won't that affect the explosions?"

Zimsky shook his head, clearly disgusted. "Yes, and what if the core is made of cheese? These are all best guess, Commander. All science is best guess."

The commander looked first from Zimsky to Serge, then to Josh.

All Josh could do was nod. In this case Zimsky was right. It wasn't something scientists liked to admit, but it was right.

"So," Iverson said, "my best guess is 'you-don't-know.' "

With that he turned and headed for the door. There wasn't a thing Josh, or any of them could say to that, because in essence, he was exactly right. They just didn't know.

And wouldn't until they got there, if they got there.

Twenty minutes later they decided on taking the five two-hundred megaton bombs, simply for the reason that it sounded right, and it was their best guess at what they were going to need, and it looked like the most payload the ship could safely carry.

And since time was short, they had to pick something.

The next morning, before the sun was even up over the rock bluff to the east, Josh entered a building that hadn't even existed four days before, and climbed up on a platform that ran beside a mock-up of the ship's cockpit area. The mock-up was painted a bright white, and with the bright lights on the entire area, Josh was glad he'd brought along an extra bottle of water for the first days of simulations.

The cockpit area was larger than Josh had expected it to be, and could easily seat the six of them. The side was cut away for easy access and viewing, and a control central area had been built facing the open side.

Stickley and three of her people were working over that control area, ignoring everything else around them.

Colonel Childs and Commander Iverson were already in the two front seats, running checks of the instruments and computer panels in front of them. Iverson was on the right, Childs was on the left.

Zimsky was in the rear left seat, Serge in the rear right seat, and Brazzleton in the seat between them. All of them had computer panels around them, and keyboards in front of them.

One empty seat remained, in the center and just behind the two pilots. That was Josh's seat. And from the looks of that space, the way the ship closed in around him, the way the computer screens framed the seat just below eye level, he was going to have trouble getting in there.

He could feel the sweat starting to form on his forehead as he tried to ignore his fear of small, tight places. He had always thought his claustrophobia was stupid, and had ignored it most of his life. But now, facing that capsule, it was hitting him hard.

"Ready for you, Dr. Keyes," Commander Iverson said.

Colonel Childs glanced around at him and smiled. He wasn't sure if her smile made him sweat more, or feel better. He sure didn't want to make a fool of himself in front of her.

Josh nodded to the pilots. He turned and stepped toward General Purcell who had just arrived.

"You called," the general stated.

"General," Josh said, taking a deep breath and just blurting out what he was thinking, "you need to replace me. I can't be on the crew."

"Why's that?" Purcell asked, frowning.

Josh didn't really know what to tell him. "Well, first off, I don't do well in groups. I never was a locker room kinda guy. And really, between Zimsky and Commander Iverson, I think you have all the leadership you need down there."

General Purcell had the decency to not laugh. He just stared at Josh, until finally the look was too much.

"Annnd . . . I'm claustrophobic," Josh said. "Have been since I was a kid. I can't get in an elevator without breaking into a cold sweat."

"Son," Purcell said, patting Josh on the back like he was Josh's father, "I was afraid of bullets, but they still sent my ass to Vietnam. Keep up the good work."

With that the general walked off.

Josh turned and stared at the open seat in the mock-up. It looked like he had no choice. He was the leader of this mission, and there was no getting out of it.

He forced himself to take a deep breath, then a drink of water. "Okay, Josh," he said to himself. "Can't be any worse than getting into an airplane," he thought as he strode toward the open chair in the mock-up.

It turned out, it was, but he made it, somehow.

With everyone in place the simulation began. Stickley and some engineers were at the controls in the booth and every "terranaut" in his or her place on the simulation ship, which began to shake.

So far, they were doing fine. But how long this smooth sailing, or digging as the case was, would last would depend on how well they handled the problems Stickley was going to throw at them next.

"Speed sixty miles per hour," Beck called out. "All systems are green."

Stickley gave a small nod, and the green lights turned red on Zimsky's panel. The ship vibrated more violently.

"Feedback in the resonance tube," Zimsky called out from his station.

"Talk to me, gentlemen," Commander Iverson said, his voice firm and level.

Beck knew that the commander was trying to build a working team, where communications was the key.

Right now the Commander wanted to know if he needed to slow down or not.

"We are losing structural integrity," Serge said.

Beck glanced back as the mock ship started to rock and bounce around.

"It's not feedback, Zimsky," Brazzleton said.

"Advise me, people," the commander shouted over the noise.

Beck glanced at her readouts. Red lights were flaring everywhere. And they were still shoving ahead at over fifty miles per hour through solid rock.

"Brazz?" Josh said, "for God's sake, make the call!"

"I should make the call," Zimsky said.

If Beck could have belted the stupid little scientist right at that moment, she would have.

"What part of talk to me do we not understand?" Commander Iverson shouted, glancing over his shoulder.

Suddenly there was a loud bang, a hard jar that tossed the crew hard against their seat belts, and the mock-up tipped up and froze, leaving them hanging from the belt looking down at the nose of the ship.

There was a very painful pause, then Stickley loudly tossed her headset onto the control panel outside the mock-up control area, and stepped up to look at them hanging there.

"For the twenty-second time in a row, everyone on Earth is dead."

She let that thought sink in for a moment, then went on. "Let's all take a little quiet time, and then y'all are going to try this again."

With that she turned and stepped off the platform and moved over to the table with food and drink, leaving them hanging in the position they had ended up. Beck knew that leaving them literally hanging was a good technique, and rammed home the idea that if they screwed up like that ten miles deep, that was where they were going to die, right ahead of the rest of the planet.

Beck glanced around and up at where Josh was hanging in his seat, looking very uncomfortable as he held himself in place with both hands on his computer terminal. She smiled at him, and then went back to staring ahead, trying to make the best of a very uncomfortable position. She had no doubt this wouldn't be the last time they were going to fail. That was the point of these simulations.

But she desperately wanted this crew to be ready when the ship was ready. And from the way things were going, she wasn't sure that was going to happen.

The meeting had been called by Stickley for one simple reason. As the entire crew got together, she looked at them and asked, "Where's our launch site?"

The last two days of simulations had gone better

than the first try. At least now they were getting deeper and deeper into the planet before they died. For some reason, Josh was finding that encouraging.

Also they were starting to work better as a team. Over the last few days of simulations Josh had wanted to kill Zimsky at least ten times, but now he had the scientist under control, to an extent, and working with them, instead of against them.

Brazzleton pulled up images on the large screen in the mission control area, and began cycling through maps of different world regions.

"We need to cut our actual digging time as much as possible." Zimsky said. "Start somewhere low."

"So we go to Death Valley," Dr. Brazzleton said.

Zimsky snorted. "Waste anything but time. We're digging a hole, why not start with a hole?"

"The ship was built for a desert launch," Brazzleton said, glaring at his enemy.

Zimsky moved over and punched up a map on the big screen, then brought it in closer and closer. Josh knew instantly what he was thinking, and didn't much like it.

"Marianas Trench in the Pacific," Zimsky said, pointing at the map that was now showing a topographical image of the ocean floor. "Six miles below sea level, gives us a running start. The ship has a finite amount of energy, we need to conserve every minute of it we can."

"Great," Brazzleton said, disgusted. "So I have to make the damn ship waterproof, too?" And he stormed out of the room. The others followed him out each returning to their specific tasks at hand.

Josh was at work on one of the ship's components when Beck entered his lab later that day. There were a dozen techs working in the lab, some of them top scientists from around the world. He couldn't believe he had a staff of that caliber under his command. Such a thing would have been laughable a month ago.

Of course, so would the Earth's Core stopping its spin.

She said she had come to see what he was up to, and he wasn't quite sure how to take that. But he figured he'd just show her. He did better with science than with women. It was less scary. He took her up to a flat screen that was about the size of a car windshield. It would end up being the front panel ahead of the pilots, to give everyone in the cockpit area a sense of seeing ahead, even though it was only a screen.

"I invented this," Josh said, pointing to the panel. "It's how you're going to steer underground."

On the screen were somewhat fuzzy images of people, furniture, and a room, all displayed in a type of 3-D image.

"Not very good reception," Beck said, staring at the screen.

Josh laughed. "We're looking through three feet of lead fifty yards away. It ain't bad."

She glanced at him and smiled.

"It's like a CAT scan at a hospital," Josh said, "but souped up. I invented it for deep-earth surveying. One day the Department of Defense showed up, bought my research, paid off my student loans, made me a consultant."

Josh sat down and started fiddling with the electronic antennas, examining them as he talked, trying to clear up the reception a little.

Beck sat beside him. He was surprised that her presence that close was very comforting.

Josh went on telling her how this had come about. "Then they called me when the pacemakers quit, and boom, I'm Apocalypse Boy."

She laughed and glanced at him. "Apocalypse Boy?"

"I'm having tee shirts made up," he said.

"Hats sell better."

Josh laughed and kept working on the antennas while he talked. "Hey, I'm the guy who discovered the world was going to end, and now, for some ungodly reason, I'm the guy in charge of stopping it. I'm a little ragged around the edges."

She nodded and said nothing. Then she smiled and pointed at the screen. "This is pretty cool."

Josh let the compliment get inside. For some reason it made him calmer, more relaxed.

Then, as he watched, she reached up and twisted an

116

antenna, working it to the right and up slightly. The image on the display became slightly clearer.

Josh looked at the image, then at what she had done, then at her. "Is there *anything* you can't do?"

"I can't burp on cue," she said, smiling at him.

For the first time in what seemed like a lifetime, he laughed. He actually laughed.

chapter ten

JOSH WAS IMPRESSED AT HOW FAST THE SHIP WAS COMING TO-gether. Every time he had reason to go into the big hangar, he did. Right now, from all reports, the ship was three quarters covered in the Unobtainium of Dr. Brazzleton. And since the only way to cut and form it was with the liquid nitrogen, the area around the ship seemed to be constantly surrounded in a swirling fog. Today, Josh was also finally seeing a fully animated schematic of the ship's interior.

The ship itself was looking like a type of segmented worm, with a number of compartments, all working on their own.

"We're powered by this experimental miniature nu-clear reactor in the chamber right behind the cockpit," Brazzleton said, pointing to the section as the schematic worked its way back through the ship. The entire crew had gathered in the main hangar for this virtual tour, and Beck was standing beside Josh, also staring at the screen.

It seemed that more and more over the past few days, Josh had found Beck standing beside him, or eating lunch with him, or sitting next to him in meetings.

And he had done the same in return. If she was sitting alone, he joined her. Her company was giving him extra strength and confidence. He had no idea why she was hanging around with him, but he sure wasn't going to question it until long after the mission was done and the world was saved.

The image on the screen in front of the crew moved down through the ship, showing them what would be inside the shell being put together in the hangar behind them.

"Living quarters, science lab, and the bombs are here in the fifth compartment," Brazzleton said. "Weapons control for the nukes is in the last compartment here."

"Everyone followed his demonstration intently.

"Up to a forty-five degree angle, each compartment is kept level by gyro-controlled gimbals." Brazzleton continued.

The animation showed a section of the ship jettisoning. "Any section breaches," Brazzleton said, "bulkhead doors engage automatically, it seals up and ejects."

"That really the best option?" Serge asked.

Josh had felt the same way the first time he had heard about the plan of separate compartments in the long, thin ship. But for the life of him he couldn't come up with anything better.

"One damaged compartment degrades the entire hull under the pressure we're going to be dealing with," Brazzleton said. "Something springs a leak, we cut it loose."

"What if the damaged compartment is in the middle?" Beck asked.

Brazzleton glanced around, then shrugged. "I'm working on that."

"General Purcell would like to see you in Mission Control," an officer said to Josh.

Josh pushed himself out from under the display screen he had been working on, and glanced at his watch. Three in the morning.

Around him dozens of scientists, engineers and techs were still working in this lab. He had no doubt they were only a few of the hundreds working on this base right now. On this kind of project people got sleep where they could, when they could, and time of day meant very little.

Off to one side of the main Mission Control headquarters was where Rat had set up shop. The overall lights in the room were dark, but there were at least five techs working at screens in the main area. General Purcell was standing behind Rat.

Rat had built a computer circle around his chair, leaving only a small opening to get in and out. Data, images, films, were constantly flowing over the screens around Rat, making him look at times like he was sitting inside a light show of colors.

Josh moved up beside General Purcell and stared at Rat's main screen. It showed a very complicated series of commands and codes, all static and waiting for a blinking green Engage button to be pushed.

"What am I looking at?" Josh asked.

"Virus-bot," Rat said, his fingers flying over the keys of a board to his left. "Computer virus that'll seek out files anywhere on the Web that contain keywords we designate, and wipe 'em."

Rat shrugged and glanced back at Josh and General Purcell. "Back in ninety-nine, a primitive version was used on the German Internet." He pointed at the screen. "This is my kung-fu, and it is strong."

General Purcell nodded and glanced at Josh. "And hopefully we'll have media containment."

Josh knew all this had to be done, but wasn't sure how he felt about it completely. "Well, I'm pleased, yet incredibly creeped out at the same time."

Rat shrugged. "It won't work forever. Once this stuff reaches critical mass, this will be like a Band-Aid on the Hoover Dam."

"We just need a few more weeks," General Purcell said. "Do it."

Before Rat could move, Josh raised his hand. "People should know. It's the end of the world. People should have a chance to take care of things, go to the Grand Canyon, get married. Am I the only one it's killing to keep this secret?"

Both Rat and General Purcell stared at him for a moment. Josh could tell they both agreed with him, at least in part.

Finally General Purcell broke the uneasy silence. "The President wants people to live out what may be the last few weeks of their lives with dignity. There is no dignity in panic and flames and riots," the general said. "Now, do it please, Mr. Rat."

Rat nodded and hit the engage key. All his computer screens blinked and then went back to doing what they were doing before.

General Purcell nodded, turned, and left.

Josh and Rat were silent for a moment. All Josh could do was think about how he had just been a part of launching a massive computer virus onto the Web. That was not something he would have ever thought himself possible of doing just three weeks before.

"That guy reminds me of my dad," Rat said as the door to Mission Control closed behind the general.

"Yeah, and mine," Josh said, smiling. The guy actually did remind him of his dad. Weird that he had never thought of that before now.

"Hey, Doc," Rat said, turning back to his screens, "ever hear about Project Destiny."

"No," Josh said, his heart suddenly pounding.

"So I'm doin' this research on every deep Earth project like you asked, just grabbing data, and I bonk into a reference to a Project Destiny. All records deleted."

"So it's a dead end?" Josh asked, both relieved and disappointed.

"Silly rabbit," Rat said, smiling at him, "*delete* is for kids. Somebody hosed the data, but I found some. Project Destiny is deep earth, skunkworks, it's secret government mojo."

Josh had figured as much, but that still didn't answer most of his questions. "Can you dig?"

"I can dig," Rat said, laughing.

"Then dig it out," Josh said. "All of it. And don't tell anyone."

Josh and Rat executed the secret handshake they devised for times just like this. Then Rat turned back to the screen to get to work.

Josh turned and headed for the door that lead back to his imaging systems. He still had a lot of work to do before this night was over, and worrying about a now dead secret project that Zimsky had been involved with was not a very high priority.

Yet still it bothered him. And he was glad that maybe, with Rat's help, he might find out what exactly it had been.

He glanced at his watch. Three-twenty in the morning. He had to be showered and back in the simulator at seven. Lots of time.

And not enough. Earth had a deadline and so did he.

For the first time on the project, Beck felt at home doing a task. They had been given a type of EVA suit that, if needed, they could wear. All the suits had been designed to fit each individual. The scientists weren't too pleased about the accompanying helmets, and she could tell Josh, in particular, wasn't having much fun with it. It was clear to her that he had a mild case of claustrophobia, and was fighting right through it with every new thing they did. She admired that about him. So she tried to talk him through this.

"Let me help you with that," she said to him, taking his helmet and fitting it carefully over his sweating face. "See, it's not that bad."

He took a deep breath inside the helmet, and then nodded, clearly getting through the claustrophobia.

She put her helmet on and snapped it in place. "Can you hear me?" she asked.

"Perfectly," Josh said.

"The suits are blended with Unobtainium," Brazzleton said. "They won't save us from a pressure breach, but if hot magma leaks through, we'll be okay."

Zimsky was again making trouble. "It's far too thin to work."

Beck wanted to tell him about how thin their new EVA suits were for space, but she said nothing. The fight between Zimsky and Brazzleton was not hers, and she had, so far, stayed out of it.

"It works," Brazzleton said, stepping off to one side and picking up a device Beck didn't recognize. "I've tried it myself."

"This is ludicrous," Zimsky said. "There's no way—"

Brazzleton ignited the device he had in his hand.

Suddenly Beck recognized it. A flamethrower, an old World War II type.

Flames exploded from the weapon, covering Zimsky.

The scream from Zimsky wasn't something Beck ever wanted to hear again. Both she and Josh instantly moved to turn down the volume on their comm links.

The flames covered the scientist as he dropped to the floor and rolled, screaming and flailing the entire time.

Brazzleton cut off the flame and put down the weapon, shaking his head.

Commander Iverson, who had been closest to Zimsky, bent down and unsnapped the scientist's helmet, showing the man's perfectly fine face, his eyes clinched shut in sheer terror.

There was clearly nothing wrong with Zimsky, other than maybe he wet his pants.

Beck was disgusted, and trying not to laugh at the same moment.

"I told you it works." Brazzleton said.

Brazzleton turned and headed for the dressing room to take off the suit.

Zimsky, still laying on his back, opened his eyes slowly, moving his arms around to make sure he was all right. He clearly had not been harmed.

Beck turned and helped Josh off with his helmet, keeping her back to Zimsky to make sure he didn't see her trying not to laugh.

Josh was having the same problem, also barely containing his mirth at what Brazzleton had done to his old enemy.

Serge took off his helmet, and then went and stood over Zimsky, looking down at the sprawled scientist who was still trying to recover from his ordeal.

"He really does not like you," Serge said.

Beck barely made it to the dressing area before she burst into laughter. Through the walls in the men's section, she could hear Josh laughing as well.

*   *   *

It was just after midnight when Josh decided to head up to the roof of the command center to watch the light show that was filling the sky night after night. He needed a break, his hands were cramping, and his stomach had so much acid in it he had a concession on Tums in his pocket.

He put together a cooler of beer, just in case Serge or anyone else joined him, then went up the back staircase.

The light show didn't disappoint him.

The reds and blues of the curtains of light shimmered and danced, as if to some unheard music. The media was calling it the most fantastic show in a thousand years, and were going on about how they hoped it would last.

So far there had been no mention of the fact that maybe the light show every night meant that there were problems. Big problems.

Between Rat and the government's media team, all rumors of that sort were being stopped at once, either with lies, or outright threats. The general had mentioned that a few more, even nastier measures, had had to be taken in a few instances. Josh didn't want to know about any of that. He couldn't sleep much at night as it was.

The roofs of all the new buildings had been built flat, with utility sheds and air conditioners dotting the surface. The crew had taken to going up to the roof of their building at night, when the air had cooled down, to watch the show and relax.

One of the things that had surprised him about being out West was that the air really *did* cool down at night. In Chicago and Washington, the sun going down really didn't mean anything to the temperature in the summer. But out West, when the sun went down, the temperature soon followed, even to the point that a few of the nights had been downright cold.

Tonight the air was perfect, with no wind and no humidity. He had found a lounge chair and pulled it off to one side of the roof, facing east. He must have actually dozed for a few minutes because the next thing he knew Zimsky was standing about twenty feet away, smoking and staring out over the desert.

"If you're thinking about jumping," Brazzleton said, his voice coming from near the top of the stairs, "don't let me stop you."

"I wouldn't give you the satisfaction," Zimsky said, not even turning to look at his old enemy.

Clearly neither man knew that he was there, so Josh said nothing and just listened.

"I was just trying to make a point this afternoon," Brazzleton said.

"Well, you succeeded," Zimsky said, tossing his cigarette onto the roof and grinding it out under his foot. "Congratulations."

"Zimsky," Brazzleton said, "you ever think what might have happened if you'd stayed here?"

"Yes, my social life would have suffered terribly."

"We could have built the ship together," Brazzleton said.

Josh could hear the hesitation in Zimsky, then a sigh. "Brazz, we hated each other, even when we were best friends."

At that moment Josh decided it was time to make this team actually come together one more step. Before either Brazzleton or Zimsky could say a word, Josh said, "And yet here you two are, twenty years later, standing next to the same man, in the same place. Irony, huh?"

Both of the scientists turned and looked at him as he sat up and swung around to face them. He reached over and fished in the cooler he had brought up with him. He dug out a beer and tossed it to Brazzleton, then another to Zimsky.

From the doorway, Serge came onto the roof, closing a cell phone. Josh tossed him a beer as well.

"Madeleine and the girls say hello," Serge said. "And send their love."

"What are they doing up so late?" Josh asked, glancing at his watch. It was well into the morning hours back east.

"They like to look at the night sky," Serge said, shaking his head. "They think it's pretty."

129

Josh wished there was something he could say to comfort his friend, but there just wasn't. Serge knew he was needed here, and his being here was the only chance his family, and the rest of the world had, of surviving. But that knowledge still didn't help the feeling of missing them.

"We should run simulations up here," Beck said, coming across the roof at them. "You guys actually resemble a team."

No one said a word to that.

Josh tossed her a beer, and she dropped into a chair beside him. "Thanks."

"I hate that sky," Zimsky said.

All of them looked up. How was it possible to hate something so beautiful, yet Josh felt the same way.

He looked around at the team, and then at the sky full of glistening, shifting colors. It seemed pretty lame to think that this group could change something that big.

Actually bigger.

What gave them all the ego to think they could start an entire planet's core rotating?

Josh just shook his head. Amazing conceit.

Beck patted his arm.

No one said a word.

chapter eleven

BECK FOUGHT THE CONTROLS, WORKING THE SHIP BACK ON track, only to lose it again. She had run this same scenario almost a dozen times on the pilot's simulator. It was basically a seat on gimbals that allowed her to practice piloting the ship without involving all the rest of the crew. Iverson used it a lot during the day, she used it at night. Just in case something happened to him, she had to be ready to take over the ship's piloting duties.

She fought the stick again, pushing to keep the craft on target, but again she lost it, and this time there was no recovery. There was a loud clank and the gimbals turned her sideways hard. Her panel showed all red lights.

"Damn!"

She punched the panel hard. Those red lights illuminated her failure. She punched them again.

"Crashing one ship isn't enough for you?" Iverson asked from behind her.

The voice startled her, but she hoped it didn't show. "Practice makes perfect."

"Practice all you like," Iverson said, coming up to a position on the platform beside her so that she could see his face. "It doesn't mean you're ready to sit in that chair."

The statement made her anger come back to the surface. She faced her panel and, keeping her voice level, said, "So you keep reminding me. Sir."

Iverson laughed. "I doubt you're going to listen to this, but I'll give it a shot. Being a leader isn't about ability. It's about responsibility."

"Got you, sir," she said, wishing that he would just go away. She didn't need any more of his lectures.

"No," he said, his voice soft and almost sad, "you don't. You're not just responsible for making good decisions, you have to be responsible for making bad ones. You've got to be ready to make the really shitty call."

She turned and looked at him. Clearly he was trying to tell her something, but she wasn't sure what exactly it was. "What makes you think I'm not?" She tried to take a little of the anger out of the question, but it still sounded hard.

"Because you're so damn good, Beck," Iverson said,

shaking his head. "You haven't hit anything yet you can't beat. Hell, you figured out how to save the shuttle, made me and the rest of NASA look like asses. You won again, Beck."

She was about to say something, but he held up his hand for her to stop. "But you're not really a leader until you've lost."

With that he turned and walked away, leaving her to stare after him. He honestly *did* care about her, that much was clear. Much clearer than what he was trying to tell her.

Josh could feel the days just ticking away. So far Rat and the government had been able to keep a lid on any real warnings of coming disaster. Almost everyone thought the wonderful night sky was just due to increased sunspot activity. Only two planes, that Josh knew about, had crashed due to "unusual circumstances," and very little else was making it into the national media of any country.

But there was no doubt time was running out. The ship had been finished for one day, bombs loaded, everything tested. All systems on board were go.

Now they were retesting everything as the crew struggled to get ready. There was no doubt in Josh's mind that the crew was a long ways from being fit.

They had just finished another walk-through of the

ship. The entire crew made it to the door of the big hangar as a unit, and headed across the open area at a run for the command center. In the distance Josh could see lightning, strike after strike pounding the desert.

He could also hear a distant rumbling as the thunder echoed over the flats. The air around him felt crisp, and smelled like someone had just turned on a long-unused air conditioner.

Around them the techs and soldiers locked everything down, preparing for the worst. The base had been built to withstand a lightning storm of the size Zimsky and Josh had forecasted, but Josh and the team wanted to be in the command area when, or if it happened.

General Purcell, Stickley, and Rat were gathered around a monitoring station. Rat made the displays change with his touch. The terranauts focused on the monitors. "Lightning superstorm," Josh said.

"They're popping up all over the world," the general confirmed.

"Got 'em!" Rat shouted. "Uh oh . . . Mexico City doesn't look good."

Rat's fingers flew over the keys. Then he pointed at the big screen as a half dozen pictures flashed up there, all from different angles around the city. In the distance on two of them Josh could see the coming storm.

"Oh, my God," Beck said beside him, her voice barely above a whisper.

He couldn't agree more. It was a nightmare. The entire horizon outside of Mexico City was nothing but lightning, pounding the ground in almost one big electrical wave.

And the storm was heading right into the heart of the city.

"Nothing is going to survive that," Serge said.

There was no arguing with him as far as Josh was concerned. They watched as the storm struck the heart of the city.

Buildings exploded as they were pounded with electrical energy like nothing ever seen in nature. Streets buckled and collapsed. The lightning cyclone tore through Mexico City in minutes leaving behind only smoking ruins of flames.

The silence in the control room was more intense than Josh could have imagined. For the first time they were really faced with what was going to happen to all of them very shortly.

"The planet's decaying faster than we thought," Josh said.

"It's just the start," Zimsky said. "Pretty soon we'll have EM spikes, and microwaves will break through the weak spots."

"Get that ship in the ground. Now," Purcell commanded.

"Due respect, sir," Iverson said, "we can't."

"The ship's ready," Brazzleton said.

"This crew isn't ready," Iverson said. "We go now, we will fail."

"I concur with Colonel Iverson sir," Beck said.

There was a moment of silence as they all thought about what Iverson had said. And about what was happening out there, in Mexico City, and other places around the world.

It was clear to Josh that this team was not the best, was not really ready for what they were going to face. But from the looks of what was happening on that screen, they might not have the time to get ready.

"I think Commander Iverson is missing the fact that this crew will never be ready," Serge said.

He looked around at the team and shrugged. "I lie?"

"Nope," Josh said, "I'm with Serge. Might as well send us now, it's not like we're improving."

General Purcell almost smiled. With a glance at Iverson and Beck, he turned to Stickley and nodded.

"All right, folks, pack your bags," Stickley said, "y'all are going to work."

Josh wasn't sure exactly how he expected to feel right at that moment, after all the weeks of training and hard work. But what he did feel was panic.

Sheer panic.

He took a deep breath, and fought down the urge to just shout *no!* Instead he nodded. And hoped that the rest of the crew was more confident than he was right now. They filed out of Mission Control silently. Each, no doubt with some thought of the weight of their mission—saving the planet.

Six very hectic hours later, Brazzleton's ship lifted off on a transport, headed for the south seas. Josh stood and watched it on the roof of their dorm. Twelve hours after that, Josh and the rest of the team left the Utah desert.

They transferred to a Chinook helicopter at some dark base for the last leg over the ocean.

During the trip the talking had been light, with everyone still buried in their own thoughts. Josh had tried to push aside Commander Iverson's words about this team not being ready, but Josh knew he was right. And that Serge was right in that this group of people would never be ready, at least to standards set by the commander.

What was going to be important was this team's ability to figure out the problems they faced, and find solutions. And if there was ever a group that could do that, it was this one.

The gantry for launch had been built on a huge ocean platform, starting the day after they had made the decision to launch in the trench. From all the pictures Josh had seen, it was like having a NASA launch tower floating on the water.

But the pictures were nothing to match the first sight of the thing. It was like a long, black worm hanging upside down from a scaffolding, its nose pointing down through a massive hole in the platform's floor.

Around them the night was pitch dark, and the only thing lit up was the tower and the ship. It wasn't a sight that Josh would soon forget.

The Chinook circled once and then headed for the pad on the south corner of the big platform.

The noise from their transport died out as they climbed to the deck and headed for the ship. It towered over them like a gleaming, black wall, stretching up into the night sky.

The crew stared up at their ship. It was humbling. Then Serge pulled out a bottle of champagne. "I was saving this for later," he said. "But I think this is the moment for a toast. No?" The ever-prepared Frenchman also produced paper cups and started pouring the champagne.

Josh continued to stare at the ship that they hoped could help save them all. "Shouldn't we have a name for this baby?" he asked.

"She's called *Virgil*," Brazzleton said.

"*Virgil*," Zimsky said, "as in Dante's *Inferno?*"

"Yeah, Zimsky," Brazzleton said, "I read books, too."

Josh shook his head. "Virgil, the poet who led man

through the depths of Hell? That's appropriate, I guess." He lifted his paper cup. "Here's to Virgil."

They all toasted their new ship, and Josh thought they finally worked like a real crew.

Everyone started working their way across the deck toward the ramp that led over the hole and up to the entrance into the ship through an impeller vent. Josh and Beck were going slower than the rest, lagging behind a little, taking it all in. Iverson was right in front of them.

"No flashbulbs, no press," Iverson said, shaking his head as he looked around. "Nobody cheering. Weird. Just guys going to do a job."

No one had anything at all to say to that.

"OK," Iverson said. "Let's do it." One by one they climbed into the ship.

"Come on," Beck said to Josh, pointing upward. "Look at that thing. Tell me you're not just a little stoked?"

"Yes," Josh said, "I can't wait to get into the untested ship and go to the center of the Earth with a thousand tons of nuclear weapons. Whee."

Beck laughed.

Josh was just happy to not be throwing up right at that moment. He stopped on the edge of the ramp and looked down into the dark, swirling waters of the Pacific below *Virgil*. He fished a penny out of his pocket, and tossed it into the ocean.

"Make a wish," he told Beck.

"What's that?" she asked.

"My lucky penny," he said, smiling at her.

She smiled back at him—something he decided right then that he wanted to see a lot more of—"Superstitious scientist. Great."

He took one last look at the blue sky, then the ocean surrounding them. He stood there until Beck nudged him to come up into the ship. He nodded, and headed for the entrance behind her.

Josh had been in the ship a hundred times over the last few weeks as it was being built, but it still, now, felt different. The nose of the ship was pointed straight down, but the cockpit was inside a rotating bubble that kept it level at all times.

Or at least in theory it did. Josh had spent far, far too many hours hanging from his seat belt in the simulator to believe this was going to work any better.

Serge was already in his seat, a photo of his wife and kids tucked into the panel in front of him.

Beck climbed over and into her seat and Josh did the same right behind her, making sure his belt was secure when he got there.

In front of them was his flat-vision viewscreen. It looked more like a giant windshield than anything else, and would rotate with them, staying in front of their positions, no matter how they turned inside the ship.

Josh did a quick check of his board. All systems were showing green.

He put on his headset and adjusted it.

The voice of Stickley was coming through loud and clear, checking down systems, making sure everything was in order and ready to launch. It was no wonder General Purcell had brought her from NASA for this. She was a tough taskmaster, and at her best under the pressure of a launch.

Josh flicked on the viewscreen.

It seemed as if someone had opened a shutter in front of them. Not only could they now see the ocean surface below them, but fish swimming in layers below the surface, and even the rock walls of the Marianas Trench below that.

Readouts and targeting data appeared all over the screen, telling them how far away certain items were. The image was crisp and clear, and Josh was proud of it.

Beck turned and smiled at Josh, giving him a thumbs up.

Well, so far, all was well with the world. She was impressed by the work he had done.

"Deep-Earth Control," Beck said, turning back to her panels. "This is *Virgil*, signal check."

Josh let himself relax into the prelaunch routine they had practiced so many times. It felt familiar, and calmed his nerves just enough to let him get to work, focusing on making sure that no detail was missed.

He knew that back in Utah, at the command center, they were doing the same thing, getting ready to try to save the planet.

chapter twelve

JOSH DID HIS BEST TO KEEP HIMSELF CALM AS THEY WORKED, ONE by one, through the preflight checklist. With only a few glitches that were quickly fixed, they were almost ready to go. And now, with each passing second, he became more and more nervous. Thank God he hadn't let himself eat much on the way here.

"This is Deep-Earth Control," Stickley said. "I have thumbs-up across the board."

Josh glanced around at Serge, who winked at him, then at Zimsky, who looked pale, but focused. Dr. Brazzleton also seemed to be doing fine.

"Reactor power confirmed," Commander Iverson said.

"Countdown to release on your mark," Stickley said.

Iverson nodded to Beck that she should be the one to

give the word. She glanced back at Josh, who managed to nod at her.

"Mark," she said, smiling at him before turning back to her controls.

"Gantry count," Stickley said. "Ten, nine, eight, seven . . ."

Josh braced himself. They had been warned that the jolt of the ship dropping into the water might be a little rough.

". . . six, five, four . . ."

Josh had never heard anything take so long. Why couldn't they just say, "Go!" and launch?

". . . three, two, one, release!"

There was a distant clanging on the outside of *Virgil*'s hull, then an immediate feeling of free fall.

The ship dropped.

On the screen in front of them the water rushed up.

Josh wanted to cover his face, it seemed so real, yet instead he sat there, frozen.

The impact was nothing compared to what Josh had been expecting. Instead, *Virgil* just cut smoothly into the water and kept diving, slicing downward through a large school of fish at a hundred feet.

Iverson eased back on the stick, pulling *Virgil* out of the steep plunge, and slowly worked to level the ship out a little.

Around them the bubble that contained the control

cabin moved, keeping them level. The main screen stayed in front of them.

"Five hundred feet," Beck said. "Leveling out."

Josh let go of the breath he had been holding, then worked to free his fingers from their death grip on the arms of his chair.

"Light 'em up, Beck," Iverson said.

After the decision to go in through the trench had been made, headlights had been added to *Virgil*. Beck flicked them on, illuminating the water ahead of them, helping Josh's sensors see even better using a combination of cameras and his device.

"All green," Josh reported on his board.

"All green," Serge repeated.

Zimsky and Brazzleton did the same.

"Roger that," Stickley said. "All systems go."

Josh again forced himself to take a deep breath. They were on their way, and the launch into the water, something that he had worried about for a week, had gone off without a hitch. The next big question mark was the transition between the water and the ocean bottom.

"Eight hundred feet," Beck reported.

"Gyro leveling operational," Brazzleton said.

"Hull integrity holding," Serge noted.

"I'm going to keep her nose down, about fifteen degrees and—damn," Iverson said.

The crew stopped their launch duties for a second and looked up. Iverson was staring at the main screen. Whales were all around them. Their songs echoed in the cockpit.

"They're singing to us," Beck said, her voice hushed, like she was in a church.

"*Virgil*'s resonance tubes are power up," Brazzleton said, "so they're vibrating subsonically. We're singing to them."

Josh alternated from watching the whales on the screen to watching his readouts.

Then a sudden shudder ran through the ship.

All lights remained green on Josh's board.

"Was that a whale?" Zimsky asked.

"Nope," Josh said. He showed no sign of any kind of collision on his board at all. "Depth?"

"Sixteen hundred feet," Beck said. "And plenty of room on both sides?"

"Hull integrity is still good," Serge said.

"You sure?" Josh asked as another shudder ran through the ship.

"Increase the impeller speed," Brazzleton said. "We're going to need additional control."

"Done," Iverson said.

"What was it?" Josh asked, not wanting to take his eyes off of his panel.

"An underwater earthquake," Stickley said from

146

Deep-Earth Control back in Utah. "We're tracking it here. It's a good-sized one."

"Still think the water launch was a good idea, Zimsky?" Brazzleton asked.

"We picked this location because the Crust was so thin," Zimsky said. "The downside is—" He was cut off as the ship lurched violently despite Iverson's attempts to control it.

"Lots of seismic activity!" Josh glanced around at the white faces of the crew.

Then suddenly another shudder ran through the craft, this time harder and more destructive than the last two.

"Four thousand feet," Beck reported.

"We're losing steering here," Iverson said. "Some kind of cross current."

Of that Josh had no doubt. On the screen in front of them it was clear that they were now caught in some massive underwater whirlpool, more than likely set off by the earthquakes. And it was tossing them at the rock wall of the Trench.

"Brazz," Josh said, "please tell me this is OK."

"It's all fine. Entirely normal," Brazzleton said.

"I'm trying really hard to believe you," Josh said, as Iverson fought to hold the ship head-on into the current.

"OK, people," Iverson said. "Fasten your seat belts. We're turning into the skid."

The move jammed Josh back into his seat, but then a moment later the ship settled into what seemed to be smooth sailing.

Virgil control was monitoring everything back in Utah. They saw the ship correct its course, but it was descending way too fast.

"*Virgil*," Stickley said from Command, "the walls of the Trench close in as you get deeper. You need to control your descent velocity."

"Why, thank you, Deep-Earth," Zimsky said.

"We hit a wall at this speed," Brazzleton said, "we're rabbits on a highway."

"I thought you said this thing was indestructible," Zimsky said.

"The pressure makes us stronger," Brazzleton said. "There's just not enough of it yet."

"We're at twenty-five thousand feet," Beck said. "Pull out, sir."

"Can't," Iverson said. "We're locked in."

"Twenty-six thousand feet," Beck said as the ship barely skimmed the edge of one side of the Trench.

Josh watched, not able to really help in any way. Now it was all up to Iverson and Beck. This was the reason they were on board. They were the best in these types of situations, and right now the best was what they all needed.

"Twenty-seven thousand feet," Beck said.

On the front screen the bottom of the Trench was coming up fast.

"Go to full throttle," Brazzleton said. "Engage front and lateral lasers."

"We hit bottom in ten seconds," Serge said, his voice sounding surprisingly calm to Josh.

"Not enough time for power-up," Iverson said, even though he had done exactly as Brazzleton had ordered, the instant he had ordered it.

"Give it a couple more seconds," Brazzleton said, his voice level and in control. "She'll be fine."

Those two seconds, with the sea floor rushing at them, the Trench walls passing in a blur, seemed to last an eternity. Finally Josh knew the start-up had set as the final light on his board went green.

"Do it!" Both Josh and Zimsky shouted at the exact same moment.

Iverson pounded the laser Start button.

The water in front of them suddenly erupted into a boiling mass, as the combination ultrasonics and lasers that were built to carve through solid rock moved the water out of the way faster than it could flow back.

Virgil hit the bottom of the Trench, and with a massive shake kept right on going.

For a moment Josh thought *Virgil* was going to come apart around them. The shaking snapped him back and forth.

Then Iverson got it under control, throttling back slightly for a more energy-conserving speed.

Josh let out the breath he had been holding, almost choking as he did.

He focused on his control panel. All lights were showing green.

"Switching to electron spin burst transmitter," he said.

"Deep-Earth Control," Commander Iverson said, "we are transmitting sensor data, and Colonel Childs is computing our course."

Josh glanced up at the main screen as vector lines appeared on the screen as Beck worked the course into the computer. The image on the main screen seemed clear, but showed little. Just different variations of gray, meaning the granite they were passing through was of a consistent nature. That was exactly what it was supposed to show at this point.

"Plotting through lowest density material," Beck said, "reconfiguring every five minutes."

"Hull integrity one hundred percent," Brazzleton said, his voice showing the pride of a new father seeing his baby for the first time. "Reactor power one hundred percent."

Josh liked the sound of those numbers a lot.

"All green on the bomb compartment," Serge said.

Josh liked that report as well.

"Speed is sixty miles an hour," Josh said.

"Hot damn," Beck said, the joy in her voice clear.

"We'll be through the Crust in fifteen minutes," Zimsky said, "and into the Mantle. Twenty-four hours to the Core, and then, assuming we survive—"

They all looked at him. "Assuming?" They echoed.

Zimsky just went on. "—another fifteen hours to the Inner Core, Outer Core border."

"Dr. Keyes," Iverson said, "what's that reading?"

Josh looked up at the big screen. A bunch of shadowy shapes seemed to floating ahead of them. Nothing unusual.

"Mass variants," Josh said. "Different densities than the granite around us."

"Go around it?" Beck asked, glancing back at Josh.

"No," Josh said. "The view screen is density calibrated. Anything we can't just plow through will appear black."

"Got it," Iverson said.

Beck nodded.

Josh was studying the big screen. "But what are those shapes? They almost look like animals."

Then, just as Zimsky spoke, he realized just what he was seeing.

"They *are* animals," Zimsky said. "This is a petrified bog, and it's a graveyard. For mammoths."

Virgil cracked through the edge of the bog. Around

them, suspended in all sorts of different positions, were skeletons of mammoths and other creatures, flashing past like they were standing beside a highway instead of buried miles underground.

The crew watched the incredible sight in silence. It wasn't like anything Josh might have imagined he would ever see.

As they flashed past it, Beck glanced around at Josh, a look of intense joy on her face. Then, as if not really wanting to speak aloud, she said, "I'm Neil Armstrong."

Josh understood exactly what she meant.

chapter thirteen

"TRANSITION TO THE MANTLE IN TWO MINUTES, *VIRGIL*" STICK-ley from Deep-Earth Command reported. "Can we get a status check?"

"Copy that," Josh said, glancing at his board. All systems showed clear, and in the long-range scans he could see the line marking the rock from the Mantle. Drilling through rock had been easy. They knew how to do that. What they were going to find in the Mantle was another question all together.

"We're all green on the panels," Beck said. "But it's a little warm in here."

Josh agreed completely. But he had thought it was just his nerves.

"That's because it's already twelve hundred degrees out there," Zimsky said.

"Do you have to say that?" Josh asked, turning and glaring at the scientist. "No. Then don't. Ever again."

Beck turned around and looked at Josh.

"What?" Josh asked, smiling at her. "I'm good."

Beck turned back to the job at hand. "We're about to make transition to the Mantle."

On the big screen the line showed as nothing more than a shady wall of lighter gray. Nothing more. But Josh knew it was so much more than that. This was their next big test. Would this ship be able to deal with the extreme heat and pressure of the Mantle?

Then, like a shot they were out of the dark images on the viewscreen that indicated solid rock, and into a bright, orange-and-black world.

Magma and melted minerals.

"All systems green," Beck said.

Iverson didn't seem to be having any problems with the controls, either, much to Josh's relief. In fact, after a moment, it looked like it had gotten easier for him.

Josh was amazed. It was as if they were now powering up a stream of molten lava from a volcano, and doing it without a problem.

"Exterior pressure's at eight hundred thousand pounds per square inch," Serge said. "Hull integrity still one hundred percent."

"That's my baby," Brazzleton said.

"It's as if we're diving through the memories of the

planet," Zimsky said. "But soon, we will pass from memory to madness."

Josh turned around and stared at Zimsky, who was talking into a mini tape recorder.

"Are you going to do that Carl Sagan shit all the way to the Core?" Brazzleton asked.

"I have a responsibility," Zimsky said.

"A responsibility for what?" Brazzleton demanded. "To make a book deal?"

Zimsky put his tape recorder away in disgust.

Josh turned back to his panels as Iverson said to himself, "Definitely not ready."

"No one is disagreeing with you, sir," Beck said, then turned and winked at Josh.

On the screen the image showed oranges and reds and yellows of the swirling magma of the Earth's Mantle. Never, in a million years, would Josh have thought he would see this, yet here he was. Sometimes life was just too strange.

The routine set in.

At first Josh had been almost afraid to leave his seat, but as the hours passed in the Mantle as they worked their way toward the Core, they all got up and moved around at different points. Josh was standing, talking to Serge at his station, when Beck turned around and motioned for him.

"Incoming message for you, Josh," Beck said. "From Rat."

Josh nodded. He had no idea what Rat might be sending him, but he had a hunch he should take it in the private navigation area in the second pod, right near the head and kitchen, just in case.

It took Josh a moment to get through the connecting door and into the small navigation area. He signaled for Beck to put Rat through.

Rat's voice came over the speaker, clear as a bell. "Josh, here's that EM field data you're *primed* for."

On the screen in front of him Josh saw a blur of data, none of it making any sense. Then he understood what Rat had meant by primed.

He quickly typed in a analysis program based on prime numbers, and set it to work on the data Rat had sent. The data on the screen immediately changed to words.

"Destiny still exists. Has our feeds. They are on-line and connected to us."

Josh's stomach did a flip. As if they didn't have enough trouble down here, there was the standard stupidness still going on in the government. He should have known better than to think it would end just because the world was going to end. Especially when it came to the likes of Zimsky.

His first thought was to go corner the little scientist and just pound the information out of him on threat of throwing him out into the magma. But then he had a better idea.

He sat down, and using Rat's same code, typed in, "Connected means you can get inside. Yes?"

Josh didn't need a response to that one. He knew exactly what Rat would do, and it made him smile.

By the time he got something to drink and headed back to the control area, he was chuckling to himself.

Back in the control area, Zimsky was sitting in his chair, nervously tapping an unlit cigarette on the side wall of the ship.

"What are you doing down here, Zimsky?" Josh asked, moving over and standing in front of the scientist. "You're as terrified as I am, which I didn't think was possible."

Zimsky looked at him, then shrugged, as if deciding to tell the truth for the first time in a long time. "At some point in their life, dear boy, everyone considers the question, 'What would I die to do?' Walk on the moon, for one."

He nodded to Beck and Iverson.

"A cure for cancer for another. For me, to go to the Core of the Earth, how could I be terrified? How could I not come?"

Josh had to agree with Zimsky, when he put it that way.

Iverson just shook his head and muttered, "People."

*   *   *

Two hours later Beck turned to Josh. "Can you tell me what is causing that?"

Josh looked up at the main screen. On long range there seemed to be a bubble of static showing on the image, among the swirling reds and oranges.

"Dr. Zimsky," Iverson said, staring at the blip of static that seemed to be growing with every passing moment, "you're our geophysicist."

Zimsky shrugged. "The Mantle's a chemical hodge-podge—"

"Say it with me," Brazzleton said, "I don't know."

"When in doubt," Serge said, "go around."

Beck's fingers were flying over her board, vector lines appearing and disappearing on the screen as she worked at trying to find a different course. All the lines went right into the static area.

"It's too big," Beck said, shaking her head as she kept working. "We turn too slow."

Josh kept staring at the image of static on the screen. He hadn't programmed in anything to look like that at all. Yet there it was, big as day.

"Deep-Earth Control?" Josh said into the comm link.

"Working on it," Stickley's voice came back. They saw everything *Virgil* saw, but had no answers yet.

"Okay," Beck said, glancing back at him, "anything we can't go through displays as black. What's static?"

"Nothing," Josh said.

Then it suddenly hit him what exactly he had said. "Nothing. It's empty space. I never taught the computer how to read empty space."

"*Virgil* can't fly, boys," Brazzleton said.

Just when they thought they may be in the clear, a huge silver-black sphere loomed into view.

Iverson was working to turn the ship as hard as he could, but it was clear they were still going to hit the sphere.

"Dropping speed," Beck said.

The ship shook dramatically yet again as it penetrated the sphere's hard cobalt shell, then smashed through.

Suddenly it wasn't Josh's view screen images that were filling the screen, but the camera back-up was showing only pitch darkness, with just the glow of the laser giving them any illumination.

"Lights!" Iverson shouted as they went into a free fall.

Beck snapped on the lights as Josh and everyone hung on for dear life.

"Keep the lasers going!" Brazzleton shouted from the back. "Try to take us nose in."

Josh understood exactly what Brazzleton was saying. If they could hit the bottom of whatever they were falling through, nose first, the lasers would just open a hole and they would keep moving, just as they had done in the bottom of the Trench.

But in the water, at that depth, Iverson could steer *Virgil*. In the air he couldn't.

The lights and lasers gave the empty world around them an odd look. At first Josh couldn't figure out what he was seeing, then as the ship smashed through a large towerlike object, Josh understood where they were.

Around them were huge crystals towering taller than any building in the world. And thousands of feet thick, all extending toward the middle of the space.

They were inside a giant crystal geode, miles across. It must have formed and then broken free from the Crust, floating like a bubble in the currents of the Mantle.

Virgil sliced through another crystal spire and slammed sideways into yet another, jerking Josh hard against his seat belt.

Virgil was now on what served to be the ground of this crystal, only moving down the rock slope like a toboggan over snow.

Quickly, with a few jerks that Josh was sure was going to break everything, *Virgil* stopped.

Suddenly.

Josh felt his belt strain hard against his lap and chest as he was yanked forward, then sideways, banging his arm on one control panel.

"I said go around," Serge moaned as he pushed himself back upright and started checking his boards. "Nobody listens to me."

"What the hell is this?" Beck demanded. Somehow she had stayed upright and at her controls the entire bumpy ride in. So had Iverson. It must be a trick they taught in flight school.

Josh pushed himself back square in his seat. He was going to have to ask her how she did that later.

"Whatever has us jammed up front is inside our lasers," Iverson said. He did a quick run through, then turned to Beck. "Shut them down."

"Powering down," Beck said, her fingers dancing over her board.

Josh had red lights all over his control panels, where just a few moments before had been nothing but green. The worst problem he could see in his area was the sensing systems that allowed them to see through the rock and Mantle ahead. A crystal must be jammed into it as well. It was down and useless.

"It's also inside our MRI cameras," Josh said. "We're blind if we can't fix that. And we can't talk to Mission Control."

All of them sat and stared at the images of the giant crystals towering around them. Now Josh knew what an ant must feel like crawling around inside a crystal mine. Never in his wildest dreams had he thought a place like this could exist anywhere outside of an amusement park.

"We have to go outside," Brazzleton said.

"What?" Serge said.

Josh glanced at Beck, then back at his board. He could see no other way to clear the MRI system and the front lasers. "I hate to admit it, but he's right."

"I'm coming," Zimsky said. "I need to collect samples."

The scientists were all on their feet now.

"First problem," Beck said. "The only way out of this ship is the way we came in, through the impeller outlet."

Josh knew instantly what she meant. The impeller outlet a few moments before had been spitting out hot magma.

"Which is still at five thousand degrees," Serge said.

"Right," Beck said, glancing at Josh for an answer.

He wished he had one.

"I could flush it with liquid nitrogen from the cooling system," Brazzleton said.

"The cooling system that's keeping us from roasting to death in this ship?" Josh asked, staring at the man who had designed the ship.

Brazzleton only shrugged.

"Alternatives, anybody?" Iverson asked, glancing from one scientist to another.

Josh wished he had one, but if they ever planned on getting this ship moving again, and getting out of this mission alive, let alone saving the rest of the planet, they had to go outside, into a crystal geode, floating in the Earth's Mantle.

"All right, then," Iverson said, "flush the tube, using as little of our coolant as you can."

Brazzleton nodded and headed for a panel where the cooling system controls were.

"We're actually going out?" Serge asked.

"We're going out," Iverson said.

chapter fourteen

IVERSON WAS LEADING, WITH JOSH RIGHT BEHIND HIM, AS THEY worked their way out of the ship. Josh didn't know what to expect, but a deep, overwhelming silence was not it. Around him the front lights of the ship reflected off a thousand surfaces, like they were inside a diamond. It was just weird.

And beautiful.

And deathly silent.

Iverson was about to take a step, when Josh noticed their precarious position. "Ahh! Wait!" he said as he pointed.

Virgil's nose hung over a cliff that extended at what looked like ten miles into the darkness below.

"Lights, Beck," Iverson said.

From inside the ship Beck rotated the flood lights, focusing them to the side where they were coming out of the ship.

"Amazing," Zimsky said, as he dropped to the crystal surface and looked around, his mouth open. The lights illuminated the world, flashing back a thousand reflections, almost like a mirrored fun-house at a carnival.

Josh knew how Zimsky felt. It *was* amazing. His mouth was open as well, as he stared at the shimmering white and lilac colors of crystals the size of redwood trees, illuminated for the first time ever.

"Theories, guesses, wild-ass hunches?" Josh asked, turning slowly as Brazzleton came out and stood beside them, looking stunned.

"Crystal geode, I think," Zimsky said. "Chemically bonded to a cobalt shell."

"A giant gem bubble in a cobalt cocoon," Josh said, nodding.

"Probably formed up in the Crust. An earthquake broke it loose and it drifted down to the Mantle."

Josh could just not believe he was standing there. "I'm inside a floating bubble of living crystal seven hundred miles below the surface of the Earth. Helluva day."

Iverson pointed to the tree-sized crystal that had jammed up against the front of *Virgil*. "To work."

"I'll start the cutting," Brazzleton said to him. "If you check hull integrity."

Iverson nodded and turned to make his way back along the side of *Virgil*.

Josh moved to help Brazzleton. He needed to be there to fix anything he could with the communications systems. They needed to get the MRI imaging up, or they wouldn't even be able to find their way back to the surface, let alone plant the bombs to save the planet. From what he could see, nothing in the system was damaged. Just jammed by the crystal.

Brazzleton fired up the cutting torch, and put it against the base of the crystal like he was a lumberjack sawing at a huge tree. It hardly made a mark.

"That's going to take forever," Zimsky said, watching Brazz working at the thick rock.

Josh was expecting another row to start when suddenly a flash of orange caught his attention. He looked around just as a large orange glob dropped past, hitting a crystal below the ship.

Then another went past, hitting closer to the ship.

Josh looked up, startled at what he saw in the distance of the roof of the geode.

"Zimsky!" Josh said. He tapped the scientist on the shoulder and pointed upward.

Zimsky's gaze followed Josh's finger. "We breached the cobalt shell!"

Suddenly there was an explosion as a part of the area near the hole over them broke free, sending a mass of crystal showering downward, along with a waterfall of magma. The repair team was knocked off their feet even though the impact was at least a quarter mile away. They found their footing only to be greeted by a wave of superheat that fogged their helmets.

Beck's voice came over the comm link. "Quit sightseeing guys, and get us out of here."

"This isn't working," Brazzleton said as crystals and magma started raining around them.

Zimsky glanced at the crystal jammed into the ship. "Reduce your heat, up the magnesium blend by forty percent, and increase your oxygen."

Brazzleton glanced at Zimsky, then nodded and tried again. The cutting torch went through the crystal like it was soft butter.

"All right, Zimsky," Brazzleton said, nodding. "I owe you."

Iverson swung back around from his inspection.

"Zimsky," he said, digging into the area where the communication unit had been jammed, "It's too dangerous, get inside. Beck, get ready to fire up on my mark."

Zimsky moved back inside the impeller just as Josh and Brazzleton had to duck a flying hunk of crystal the size of a car. It barely missed the nose of *Virgil*, bounced once, and shattered into a thousand pieces before disappearing out of the light over the edge of the cliff.

"Shit!" Brazzleton said. "I'm losing oxygen!"

Josh stared at the cutting. Brazzleton still had a quarter of the crystal to cut away.

"At this rate," Serge said, "we have three minutes before the lava gets to us."

Josh glanced past Brazzleton and out over the edge. The lower part of the crystal world was filling quickly with orange and red lava, rising quickly. Soon it would cover the ship, and make any type of outside repair impossible. It was already getting almost too warm for the suits. Josh knew that Beck would be monitoring the pressure.

Brazzleton struggled with the torch. "It won't work without oxygen."

Josh could tell there was still a half minute of cutting left. He took a deep breath and yanked out his oxygen tube from his suit, and stuck in into the torch oxygen feed.

"Fixed it," Josh said, patting Brazzleton on the back. "Now cut!"

He figured he could hold his breath for a half minute, maybe longer. And from the way the magma was rising, they didn't have much longer than that anyway.

Around him his claustrophobia started to kick in as his shallow breathing inside his suit became more pronounced. He tried to force himself to take slow, long breaths, to conserve the oxygen that was left, but he just couldn't do it.

It was too hot.

Too enclosed.

Too tight.

Stars swirled in front of his face as the blackness replaced the glowing crystals.

He gulped for air, but there wasn't any.

The world closed in around him.

At least, if he had to die, he was doing it in a pretty place. A place that no man had ever seen before.

The last thing he heard was Brazzleton saying, "I got it!"

Beck and Serge remained in the cockpit monitoring the rescue activity.

"Josh's vital signs are dropping!" Serge said, jumping out of his station.

Beck knew they had to get Josh inside now. All of them had to get in. The lava flow was rising at an alarming rate. Within sixty seconds it would be up around the ship. Those suits would not stand that kind of heat and pressure. They were at their limits as it was.

"Commander!" Beck shouted into the comm link. "We need you on board. Now Bob!"

On one camera she watched as Iverson yanked out

the remaining crystal from the impeller assembly. Brazz-zleton was hauling Josh back toward the entrance as fast as he could. Once they were clear of the impeller assembly, Iverson shouted.

"Beck, fire her up!"

She did as he had ordered, her fingers dancing over the keys on her panel.

"Good," Iverson said. "Impeller assembly's intact."

He turned and moved quickly toward the entrance, but then as Beck watched, a bullet-sized shard of falling crystal from the rocks above hit him, punching through his helmet like a sniper shot.

"No!" Beck shouted.

Iverson's face seemed to pucker in bewilderment as a small trickle of blood ran down his temple. Then he just sort of tipped over backward. His body tumbled off the ledge and down into a rising pool of magma.

"No! No! No!" Beck shouted, trying to stand against her seat belt, as if there was something she could do to save him.

There was nothing.

He was gone.

Brazzleton was fighting to get Josh up into the ship when on the camera Beck saw Serge step out, and yank Josh's dead weight up and into the ship, then just as quickly help Brazzleton inside.

Brazzleton shouted a moment later. "Beck, hit the lasers. Lateral and front!"

Beck yanked her gaze from the screen where she had just seen the commander killed, her fingers flying over her board as she started the lasers and buttoned up the ship at the same time. The commander was gone, but she was still here, and had a job to do.

Slowly the ship started to move.

She powered up even more, shoving the ship off the edge of the crystal cliff, like a fish slipping off the edge of a boat.

The cameras showed them hit the rising pool of hot magma. Then the imaging system came up and took over. She focused ahead, not letting herself think about the loss of Iverson, or what was happening behind her with Josh and the others.

"We are back up and running," she reported to the rest of the crew.

"Good," Serge said. "You need help?"

"No," she said.

No one else said a word.

The imaging system worked perfectly as well. The magma showed red and orange, the cobalt shell, that had held this crystal world safe until they got there, was a thin, light-gray line dead ahead.

She set the speed at sixty miles per hour, and plowed

right out of the shell and back into the relative calm of the Mantle.

Then she refigured their course and set the auto-pilot. They still had bombs to plant, and billions of people to save.

For the next five minutes, she worked over the ship's systems, taking care of red light after red light, not allowing herself to think at all about what had happened.

Finally, after there was nothing more she could do, she let out a deep breath.

She was now in command, something she had wanted for a long time, yet not this way.

Never this way. It was time to test the comm link and report back to control. She pushed the button and spoke slowly, trying to control her emotions.

"Deep-Earth we . . . have a fatality," she said, her voice so level it surprised her.

There was no response from Stickley, so she went on, not knowing what else to do.

"Commander Iverson died during EVA to make repairs," she said. "I've assumed command of the ship and will continue to do so until further orders."

She could not believe those words had come out of her mouth. Iverson could not be dead. That wasn't possible. He was bigger than life, annoying because he was usually right. And a good friend. He could not be dead.

Yet she had seen him die. His body dissolved into the Mantle of the planet.

A moment later the familiar voice of General Purcell came back. "Roger that. Good luck, Rebecca."

The only thing she could do was nod in reply.

chapter fifteen

JOSH HEARD SOMEONE MOAN.

Or maybe he was the one doing the moaning. He couldn't tell. All he knew was that the light was bright, and his head hurt like hell. Whoever was pounding on the inside of it should stop.

Slowly, he opened his eyes, trying to get the weird images to clear.

It took a moment before he saw the smiling faces of Brazzleton, Serge, and Zimsky. All of them were jammed into the small room they had designated as a med lab.

Something pricked at his arm.

"Ouch," he said.

He turned his pounding head to see Beck beside him, just finishing giving him a shot. Someone had taken off his shirt and put him in shorts and a tee shirt.

She smiled at him, and patted his arm, but he could tell her smile didn't reach her eyes. Something was wrong.

He motioned for a bottle of water and Beck handed it to him, helping him tip up his aching head for a drink. It tasted wonderful. Cool going down.

"You want the good news, or the bad news?" Zimsky asked.

"Good news," he said, staring at Beck.

"We are alive," Serge said.

"That's the best news you could come up with?" Josh asked, then coughed. At that point he realized he was sweating. "Christ, it's hot."

He looked at the others. They were all dressed far lighter than before, and all of them were sweating as well.

"That nitro we flushed out of the cooling system, we're paying for it," Brazzleton said. "It's ninety-eight degrees, and the temperature will climb at one degree an hour. I'll go adjust the compressors."

The man moved off.

"Yes, we might be able to make some improvements," Zimsky said, following Brazzleton out of the room.

"So that's the bad news?" Josh asked, trying to sit up.

Beck put a hand on his chest and kept him lying on

his back. It was good she did, since just the slight attempt had made him dizzy. At least the pain was fading some.

"No," Beck said, staring into his eyes. "Commander Iverson's dead."

Josh closed his eyes and just lay there, trying to focus on his own breathing. That wasn't possible. Not possible. Iverson had been there, beside him and alive when Josh had passed out.

How could he be dead?

"We're alive now," Beck said, her emotions clearly right on the surface. "That's what matters. The commander would want us to—"

"Don't," Josh said, opening his eyes and putting a hand on her arm. ". . . Just, you don't have to push this away. Give him a second. He deserves it."

Beck nodded.

Josh could tell that she was letting the grief for her friend come up to the surface for the first time. She shuddered, and her eyes closed.

Beside them Serge stood, silent.

Josh hadn't really known Iverson, yet had spent a lot of time with him over the past few weeks. It was impossible to imagine the man was gone. He had been so much larger than life, so much in control.

And now all of his duties shifted to Beck, who had been his friend.

That couldn't be easy, either, for her to deal with.

After a long minute of the three of them being silent, Josh said to Beck what he was thinking, "This all just feels too big, doesn't it?"

"It is because you are attempting the impossible," Serge said.

Josh glanced up at his friend.

Beck was looking at him also.

Serge shrugged. "You are trying to save the world. Six billion lives. It is overwhelming."

Josh had to agree with him there. He couldn't even imagine that many lives, and yet he was feeling responsible for each and every one right now.

"I have come to save my wife and two little girls," Serge said. "To save six billion, this is too much. But I think I am smart enough, and brave enough, to save three."

Serge took Josh's hand and shook it. "Nice job out there."

Josh shrugged. "You would have done the same thing."

Serge waggled his hand in a doubtful motion, then left with a smile at Beck.

Beck stayed seated in the chair next to Josh. She took his hand, and put her finger on his pulse to check his heartbeat.

"Hey, who's steering the ship?"

"Captain Autopilot," Beck said, holding up a small remote.

She smiled at him. "So, you're really some college professor? Not from the NSA, or the CIA, just . . ."

"Just a boring college professor," Josh said, "Wrong place, wrong time."

Beck shook her head. "What you did was the bravest thing I have ever seen."

"The lack of oxygen kept me from weeping like a little girl," he said, "as is my custom in dangerous situations."

She laughed and then brushed a strand of hair off his forehead.

Her touch felt wonderful. He wanted her to keep her hand on him for much longer.

Suddenly alarms went off.

Beck turned, and in one motion was off the chair, running for the command area.

"Breach! That's the breach alarm!" she shouted.

Josh jumped up to follow her, the sudden change of position making him dizzy. But, the dizziness passed in a half a second, and he stood, his hand on the bulkhead for support. His headache was manageable, and as long as he didn't move too fast, he was okay.

"Brazz," Beck said from command over the comm link, "the breach is in your compartment."

"Where?" Brazzleton's voice came back, clearly

stressed, since the containment doors had slammed shut, trapping him in there. "Where?"

Josh moved up and took his chair behind Beck, glad to be sitting after the short walk.

He scanned his boards. It showed the breach in that section, but not where. Weird.

"I can't localize it," Beck said. "But it's in there."

Josh flicked on an interior camera so he and Beck could watch as Brazzleton tore through the hidden areas of the compartment, finding nothing. Then, Brazzleton stood, shook his head, and walked toward the bathroom door.

He yanked open the door, letting out a large cloud of smoke.

There, sitting on the john, was Zimsky, smoking a cigarette.

"What?" Zimsky asked, looking up at Brazzleton.

Brazzleton just slammed the door and walked away.

Josh figured it was just flat amazing that Brazzleton hadn't killed Zimsky. As far as Josh was concerned, it would have been justifiable homicide.

Beck had made Josh go back to his cot to rest, but three hours later he was back up and working, helping on the repairs that still needed to be done.

Now, as the Deep-Earth Control time went past three in the morning, he was under an open panel next to

Beck's chair, soldering a lose connection back into place.

"Got it," he said, closing the panel and moving back up into Iverson's old chair so that he could sit next to Beck. She hadn't yet moved over to take the command seat. It didn't really matter, but at some point, she was going to have to, both mentally and physically.

He put the soldering iron away in the tool box on the deck at his feet. Then he looked up at her. "I'm Neil Armstrong. What was that?"

She smiled at him. "Every astronaut wants to be the first, to go where nobody's gone. But for ones my age, it's all been done. First to break the sound barrier. First into space, first on the moon. No frontiers left."

She glanced at him, and he could see the light in her eyes, the excitement back there, trying to dig its way through the grief. "Until today. Today I'm Neil goddamn Armstrong."

"I get it," Josh said.

"No," Beck said, shaking her head, her eyes focused on something far away. "I totally missed the point. I was looking at the glory and missed the other stuff. Iverson tried to tell me that." The realization was incredibly painful. "Now I've got it, whether I'm ready or not."

Josh smiled at her, remembering what she had said to him when he complained to her about being put in charge the first time he had met her.

"I'm sure the people in charge have full confidence in you."

He waited for her to catch what he had just said. It took a second, then she glanced at him, and laughed.

"That's the problem," she said, parroting what he had said to her, "I'm the one in charge."

He laughed with her, and for the first time in hours, Josh felt the mission was back on track.

Beck had managed to get a few hours sleep during the night, curled up on a mattress Josh had brought in from the bunk area. She hadn't wanted to, but he had insisted, and had promised he would stay on duty the entire time just in case she needed to be awoken quickly.

Then he had brought her a cup of coffee, and some types of rolls for breakfast after he woke her up.

Now she was wide awake, feeling better, and ready to face what promised to be their next big stumbling block, crossing from the Mantle into the Outer Core.

On long range sensors she could see a faint line. She glanced around. Zimsky was the only other one at his station at the moment.

"We're close to Mantle/Core interface," she said into the comm link. "Where is everyone?"

"We're in weapons control," Josh said, "checking the controls on the nukes."

Weapons control was the last section of the ship.

The bombs were kept in the second compartment, behind the control area, but the weapons controls were in the back, away from any of the actual bombs. The designers had figured it was safer that way.

She flicked on the camera showing Josh, Brazzleton, and Serge working over a table. On the table beside Serge was a notebook that Serge kept referring to.

"Comme ça et comme ça . . . all the detonator timers check out okay," Serge said. "Let's go place the system on the bombs."

He worked to place the timers into a foam-packed case to be taken to the ship's segment with the bombs.

Beck glanced up at the screen to see how long they had to the interface. What she saw surprised her. Hundreds of black, jagged-shaped objects were appearing on the screen.

"Black is bad," Beck said, repeating what Josh had told her. She couldn't go through anything that showed up black on the screen.

"They're scattered everywhere," Zimsky said from his station, "one hundred and twenty miles across."

"I'm plotting an evasion vector," Beck said, her fingers working over her panel. But with every new course, there was another black object.

"Oh, my God!" Zimsky said. "They're diamonds!"

Beck didn't much care what they were. "Great. Giant, hard, sharp things."

She flicked a switch, triggering the collision alarms. Then into the comm link she said, "We're on a collision course. Hold on, everyone."

One vector she had plotted showed a slight chance of success, so she tipped the ship hard that way, pushing the speed to give her more maneuverability.

The first huge, black hunk on the screen flashed past on the right.

Another was dead ahead. Beck throttled back, pulling the stick hard left, missing the next one as well. But there were a bunch more ahead.

On the monitor Beck could see that Josh, Brazzleton, and Serge were holding on, anchored in different locations around the compartment.

"Guys, we're dodging diamonds the size of Cape Cod," she said, moving to the right to pass another, "and we're not exactly nimble."

She yanked the stick back hard left, the force straining to rip her from her seat.

She managed to miss two more, then with no other option, tried to slide between the last two between her and the open Mantle. And she would have made it, too, if the one had been moving just a fraction slower in her direction, and spinning just a fraction less.

One sharp edge seemed to come out of nowhere, and grazed the side of *Virgil*.

A new alarm sounded.

The breach alarm.

Only this time she knew it wasn't Zimsky smoking in the toilet.

She had *Virgil* out into the open again, nothing black looming in front of them.

She glanced at the monitor just in time to see Josh and Brazzleton dive for the closing hatch, sliding underneath it.

Serge started to follow, then turned back, grabbed the notebook and the case that Beck knew held the detonators for the nukes, and ran for the door.

There was no chance he was going to make it, so he dove, pushing the case and the notebook under the closing door by just a fraction of an inch.

"Hold on!" Josh shouted to Serge from the other side, "we'll get the door open."

Beck did a quick check.

The breach was in the compartment that Serge was in. And it was bad.

The hull had been ruptured, and it was now only a matter of seconds before that compartment was flooded with hot lava.

On the screen Serge was working feverishly on the panel next to the door, trying to get it to open for just enough time for him to get through.

Beck worked her end, going so far as to get ready to override the ejection system altogether.

On another camera Josh and Brazzleton were working on the other side of the door, on the panel there. But it was clear that the ship's overall ejection system had Serge trapped.

From everything she could tell, the wall was going to collapse in less than three seconds.

"Beck, override the ejection system!" Josh shouted.

Her hand went to the button.

And paused.

Behind her Zimsky said, "A damaged compartment weakens the whole ship."

She desperately wanted to push that button. But she knew she couldn't.

She knew she didn't dare.

She didn't dare risk the entire mission to save the life of one man.

"Beck!" Josh shouted. "Override the damn door!"

Her hand stayed poised over the button.

Shaking.

At that moment the wall behind Serge bulged inward, and then groaned.

It was too late. Far too late.

If she pushed that button Josh and Brazzleton and the entire ship would be lost.

"Serge, hold on!" Josh said, fighting the panel. "Almost there!"

The wall broke, letting in the hot magma.

185

Serge was engulfed at once, his scream echoing through the comm system.

The next instant the camera in that compartment went dark.

On the other camera, Josh slumped against the floor in bitter defeat. He ripped his headset from his head and smashed it against the wall.

Beck glanced at the main screen, then watched on sensors as the automatic ejection system released the damaged compartment, taking the essence of Serge with it.

The ship adjusted automatically as it was designed to do. She did a quick check to make sure everything was green, and nothing was coming at them.

"That's it. Over." Josh said, his voice managing to not break, but only barely.

Beck watched as Brazzleton picked up the case and notebook that Serge had given his life for.

Josh was sitting on the floor, shaking his head. "He was the only one who understood how the nukes were wired."

"Josh, man, look," Brazzleton said, holding the notebook in front of the grieving man. "The guy died getting us this stuff. It's gotta mean something."

Josh looked up at Brazzleton, then nodded and took the notebook. Beck was impressed just how strong Josh was.

Josh opened the book and turned to show it to Brazzleton. "We have to figure out how to work five hydrogen bombs, from a handwritten notebook." He took a deep breath.

"In French." Brazzleton looked closer at the open page of the book, then shook his head.

Beck made herself focus on her board, and the course ahead. They didn't have far until reaching the Outer Core, and if these lives lost were going to be worth something, she had to focus on what was ahead, not what had just happened.

And not her decision.

Iverson's words echoed through her mind. She wouldn't know what it would be like to be a leader until she had to make the shitty decisions. Well, now she knew, and she didn't like it.

Ten minutes later, Zimsky had gone, and Josh came in and sat in his seat.

Beck could feel the weight that had come in with him. The sadness. And she knew how he was feeling. She had lost Iverson, now he had lost Serge. The price of this mission was getting very, very high.

But nowhere near as high as the price failure would cost.

Josh said nothing for a moment, then he looked at Beck's control panels. The readouts were not what he expected. "Did you reset the overrides?"

187

"I never pushed them," she said, turning so that she could look him directly in the eyes. That was the only way she was going to get past this. She had to confront her decision.

"You let him die?" Josh said, his voice low and angry.

Beck did not look away from the glaring intensity. "I had to."

"You killed him!" Josh shouted right in her face.

And she shouted right back. "You want me to feel any shittier about that than I do? Not possible! That was my decision. Could *you* have made it?"

Josh took a step back and stared at her.

"Could you?" she demanded.

"Yes, I could have!" he shouted at her. "If you had hit that switch I could have pulled him out!"

"Get over yourself. Fate or God—" Beck said.

"You leave God out of this!" Josh interrupted.

"Serge died so we could complete our job!" Beck finished.

"Oh, that's right," Josh said, "the job of saving the world."

"Not everybody in the world," Beck said. She picked up the picture she had taken from Serge's control panel and flipped it at Josh.

He caught it and looked at it, pain washing over his

face as he saw the smiling faces of Serge's wife and daughters.

"Just three of them," Beck said.

Josh put the picture on his panel, spun, and left.

Beck turned slowly around to face the big screen.

Then, as hard as she could, she pounded the arms of her chair over and over.

"Shit! Shit! Shit!"

chapter sixteen

JOSH STOOD OUTSIDE THE COMMAND AREA, WAITING, TRYING TO get himself together. He couldn't believe that Serge was gone. It wasn't possible. The man had been such a huge part of his life for so many years, that not having him to talk to seemed out of the question.

And having Beck admit that she had let him die because she had had to save the ship was another hard fact to swallow.

Josh had gone back to a terminal in the second compartment and rerun the computer records of the incident, just to see for himself how Serge could have been saved.

As it turned out, Beck was right.

She had set the doors to be released on the tap of a key, then had not hit the key.

He had to play that recording three times before he could admit that fact. Serge had been doomed the moment he went back for the detonation devices and the notebook. As Beck had said, he had given his life for the mission, and Beck had made the hard decision, also for the mission.

Otherwise, if she had been one ounce weaker, he, Brazzleton, everyone on the planet, would be dead. Of that there was no doubt.

Now he stood in the corridor outside the control area, sweating in the heat, trying to get up the courage to go back to his job, to face forward and do his friend's memory justice by making this mission work. By saving Serge's family.

"Virgil," Stickley's voice came in over the comm link, "you're about to cross over from the Mantle to the Core. Are you good to go?"

A moment later Beck's voice came back. "Ready as we'll ever be, Stick."

"Where's Josh?" Brazzleton asked.

"Right here," Josh said, stepping out of the passageway and into the command area of the ship. He stepped past Brazzleton and Zimsky and Serge's empty chair and took his seat.

Beck glanced back at him, sweat dripping down the side of her face. She was still in her seat instead of Iverson's.

Josh nodded and smiled at her, telling her, without saying a word, that he now understood, and he was behind her one hundred percent.

Her eyes lit up, and she smiled slightly. "Thanks," she mouthed without really saying the word.

"Deep-Earth Control," Beck said, turning back to face the screen and her controls, "we are all present and all green."

On the main screen Josh could see the faint line that indicated the interface between the Core and the Mantle. As *Virgil* crossed through it she began to shake. But it wasn't anything she hadn't been built to handle.

Suddenly they were in what the screen was showing as bright, orange light. There were swirling colors all around them, and the light was almost too bright to stare at.

Josh brought the brightness of the main screen down so that they could look at it without squinting, yet allowed Beck and everyone to see exactly what they were facing.

"We just got a huge speed jump," Beck said. "We're at ninety-five miles an hour. One-ten . . ."

"One thirty, one hundred and forty miles per hour." Josh said, watching the speed on his board go up.

"How you holding up, *Virgil?*" General Purcell asked over the comm link.

"Our speed has jumped," Josh said, "because the

192

density of the core is different from our estimates. It's lighter than we thought."

"So much for best guesses," Brazzleton said. "Have we actually ever guessed anything *right* yet?"

"I'm fine with this," Beck said. "At this speed we'll reach the Inner Core in a little over five hours. We finally bought some luck."

"Braz," Zimsky said, his voice strangely low, "could you please punch the new Core density into the equations for the nuclear detonation?"

Josh suddenly had a very strong sinking feeling in the pit of his stomach. He turned around and looked at Brazzleton. "Please tell me it's enough."

Brazzleton shook his head.

Josh turned back and did the same calculation, running it quickly on his board. The word "Failure" appeared on the top.

"You're telling me the thousand megatons of nuclear warheads we hauled here aren't going to cut it?" Beck asked, looking back at the scientists.

Josh couldn't believe it either.

He ran it again.

And then again.

Each time the math didn't lie.

"This Core material's too thin," Zimsky said. "The energy waves from the explosion won't spread far enough. They'll just bleed away into nothing."

"Please tell me this is not happening," Josh said, staring at the world "Failure" blinking in red letters on his screen. "Deep-Earth Control, we're sending up data. Do you reach the same conclusions?"

"*Virgil*," Stickley said, "we're still working, but it looks like you're on the money. Your bombs are not going to do the job."

"That's it," Zimsky said, sighing. "We go home."

Everyone turned and stared at the scientist.

"Our commander is dead," Zimsky said, "our weapons specialist is dead, our Weapons Control Systems are gone, we don't know if we can even arm the nuclear devices, and our plan to fix the Core no longer works. We've failed, and we go to the alternative."

There was an alternative?

"General," Zimsky said, breaking into the link to Deep-Earth Control, "this is Dr. Conrad Zimsky. Destiny is go."

They just continued to stare at Zimsky.

"What's Destiny?" Beck asked.

"Project Destiny," Josh said, before Zimsky could answer, "some deep Earth research project they buried even from us. Now we know who buried it."

The terranauts could hear commotion at Virgil Mission Control. Apparently Stickley knew nothing about Project Destiny either. "It's a weapon," Josh said, glaring at the scientist.

"It's a device," Zimsky corrected. "Deep Earth Seismic Trigger Initiative, DEST-INI, Destiny. We had reason to believe that our enemies were building a weapon that could generate targeted seismic events. They would be able to create massive earthquakes under our territory, with no way for us to tell who did it."

"So?" Josh asked, disgusted at everything he was hearing.

"So we built one too," Zimsky said. "They did it first, I did it better. I beamed super-high electromagnetic energy waves down deep Earth fault lines."

"Zimsky," Brazzleton said, "I didn't think you could sink any lower. But this . . ."

"Did you create any earthquakes?" Josh asked.

"Nothing of any significance," Zimsky said, shrugging and wiping the sweat from his face with a towel. "So I stopped testing a few months back."

"So you want to scratch this mission for a failed piece of crap experiment?" Brazzleton asked. "How do you think Destiny could even touch the Core?"

Zimsky again wiped his face with the towel.

Josh knew exactly why. "Because it already did. This isn't a fluke. We did this. We stopped the planet's heart."

"It wasn't us, dear boy," Zimsky said. "It was the other side."

"Us-them," Brazzleton shouted at Zimsky. "Our side—the other side! Who cares. We all did it!"

"You keep saying the Core is too big to be affected by anything short of nukes," Beck said, looking puzzled.

"The Core is an engine," Josh said. "Throw a small wrench into a big engine, you can still stall it."

Beck shook her head. "Deep-Earth Control, this is *Virgil*. We require clarification on the status of Project Destiny. Why weren't we notified of this, sir?"

"Because you didn't need to know, Colonel," General Purcell responded.

Josh hated that. And right at this moment in time hated all governments and their stupidity.

"You may not like this," Purcell went on. "I may not like it either, but it's my job, and I do it for my country. If we don't develop these devices, someone worse will, and they'll use them against us."

Josh just shook his head, the sweat dripping down his neck and arms.

"You have my word," Purcell said, "that no one, no one, in this administration had any idea this could happen."

Josh could not believe the man had actually said that. It sounded like something the president would say in covering his ass to get reelected. Of course, now there was never going to be another election, or another administration, or even any more human beings to form stupid governments.

"So the device that helped kill the planet is your backup plan?" Brazzleton asked.

"You think we'd put all the world's eggs in this one tin basket?" Zimsky asked. "Please! We had to have backup. An electric shock can stop a heart, it can also restart one. Destiny will work. It has to."

"No, it won't work," Josh said. "Fire that thing again, with the core already stalled, you'll terminally destabilize it."

"There's a marginal risk, I grant you," Zimsky said, "but under the circumstances . . ."

"Every volcano on the planet will blow," Josh said, amazed at the stupidity of the man. "It'll cause earthquakes big enough to rip us to pieces."

"Dr. Keyes," General Purcell said from Deep-Earth Control, "I'm afraid it's all we've got. I have orders from the president. Come home, *Virgil*. We're going to plan B."

"What about plan C?" Josh asked, glancing at Beck. "We continue on. We restart the Core, somehow. If we don't do it, you fire Destiny."

"I can't wait for you to get out of there," General Purcell said.

"Then don't wait," Josh said. "We fail, you fire Destiny."

"If we're still down here when they fire that thing the shock waves will wipe us out!" Zimsky said, his voice almost a shriek. "We'll barely make it if we turn back now."

"To save every life on Earth?" Brazzleton said, nodding to Josh, "that's a shot worth taking, isn't it?"

"Not every life," Josh said, glancing at the picture of Serge's family on his board. "Just three."

Beck looked at him and nodded her agreement.

Zimsky was shaking, he was so upset. His voice was high and manic, like a crazy man. "This is insane! You're a bunch of suicidal morons, hell-bent on your own martyrdom. I can't believe I'm stranded in this floating septic tank with—"

He paused to take a breath, his eyes wide and panicked.

"You people may think you have nothing to lose, but I will not do this! I will not!"

Brazzleton, in one smooth move, unbuckled his seat belt, stood, took a step toward Zimsky, and slugged the man across the chin.

Zimsky went limp, his eyes rolled back into his head.

Brazzleton rubbed his knuckles and then shrugged at Josh, moving back over to his seat.

"Virgil!" General Purcell said, "I am telling you right now. We're going to fire Destiny and we need to do so as quickly as possible. If you're still down there, it will destroy you."

There was silence for a moment.

Josh looked at the cold-cocked Zimsky, then back at the intent look on Beck's face.

"Rebecca," Purcell said, "I'm not talking as your commanding officer, but as your godfather. I'm asking you, begging you, please don't make me have to do this."

Josh watched as Beck's shoulders slumped. The man was putting far, far too much pressure on her, as if this decision didn't have enough pressure as it was.

She took a deep breath, then turned to face Josh and Brazzleton.

"Your call, Commander," Josh said.

She knew where he stood.

Beck looked at him for a moment, letting his words sink in. She straightened her back, taking on the role as commander. Then she glanced at Brazzleton, who nodded his agreement.

"Majority decision," Beck said to Deep-Earth Command. "We're going in."

Then a second later she added, softly. "I'm sorry, sir."

"Get back to work, people," Stickley said to the cheering that Josh could hear in the background. "We've got soldiers in the field."

chapter seventeen

"OH, SHIT!" RAT SAID, STARING AT HIS SCREENS. WHAT HE HAD feared would happen, what Josh had warned him might happen, was happening.

Alarm bells started ringing all over the Deep-Earth Command area, bringing Stickley and General Purcell running up behind him.

"What's happening?" Purcell demanded.

Rat didn't answer as his fingers worked the keys, pulling up more and more data.

"Status. What is that!" Stickley asked, pointing to a screen that showed a bright red area over a part of the central part of the United States and Canada.

"It's the EM Field Monitoring station," Rat said, his fingers still flying over the keys. He couldn't just trust one monitoring station, he had to make sure. He needed more information on what was happening. "This one tracks EM Pulses."

The red blob on the screen seemed to be bigger, covering more land than he wanted to think about.

"Oh, shit, oh, shit, oh, shit," Rat said, as more and more screens confirmed what the first one did. This wasn't good. Not good at all.

"Just talk, Mr. Rat," the general said, patting his shoulder in an attempt to calm him down. "There's a good lad."

"The EM field's been getting pretty unstable," Rat said, "So there's this hole."

He pointed at the giant red spot covering a large area of Michigan and the Great Lakes, including Chicago.

"What does that mean?" Stickley demanded.

"Those invisible microwaves Josh was talking about," Rat said. "They just found a hole and are pounding the ground."

"Oh, no," Stickley said.

"Oh, no, is right," Rat said as he worked over his boards, fighting to bring up local television stations in the areas affected. He had a hunch he wasn't going to like what he saw.

On a placid part of Lake Michigan, two fisherman sat in a small, wooden boat, slowly clicking away on their reels as they brought in their line, trying to lure the fish to bite.

Danny Sterns, in the nose of the boat, owned the local grocery store, and this was his regular day off. The other man, his best friend, Hank Davids, had come just for the day, just to fish. They had been playing in and fishing on this lake since they were both boys. Now, every chance they got, they dug out the old boat, bought worms from Drakes Hardware Store, and headed for the lake with a cooler of beer and sandwiches.

Today was one of the more beautiful days they had could remember in years. The weather was warm, but not hot, and even the bugs were down.

The morning had gone well, so far at least, with a nice sixteen inch rainbow among the catch. Danny had gotten that one, and Hank had stated that he wasn't leaving until he caught one even bigger.

Along the shore of the tree-lined lake a jetski went past, its driver young and ignoring the fisherman as he chopped the water on what would otherwise be a calm lake. A developer had bought a section of lake front to the north and built condos on it, bringing in all types of people that neither Hank nor Danny wanted on their lake.

"Goddamn jetskies," Hank said, as the boat rode over the wake.

"Hate the damn things," Danny said, keeping his eye on his line.

"I'd ban the bastards," Hank said.

"Nah," Danny said, laughing, "just shoot 'em and have done with it."

Hank laughed as well, liking that idea.

Then, just as he was about to say something about getting his grandfather's old rifle, the jetski exploded in a fireball.

"What the—" Danny said.

"Holy shit," Hank said, tossing his pole into the bottom of the boat and turning around to start the engine. He doubted the kid on the ski could survive that explosion, but they needed to go find out.

Around where the jetski had exploded, the water started to steam and boil, angry clouds shooting up into the air like a geyser had erupted under the water.

"Get us out of here!" Danny shouted.

Hank didn't have to be told twice. He gunned the boat and headed for the dock, as behind them the line of boiling water and steam rushed at them.

It was the longest twenty second ride Danny had ever taken as he stared behind them, watching the boiling steam and water gain on them.

Hank jammed the boat into the dock, and Danny sprang out, rope in hand like he was a kid again.

Hank grabbed the dock and jumped as well.

It sounded like a freight train was bearing down on them. The ground was shaking, the dock swaying.

Both of them were halfway down the wooden surface when whatever was causing the water to boil caught them.

Neither of them had even an instant to feel the intense pain as they both exploded and then vaporized under the intense heat.

On the shore the forest exploded, tree after tree, sending cannon-like sounds over the surrounding land as the forest was vaporized. The overwhelming destruction headed out of the once idyllic forest and set its course for the nearby city of Chicago. The unsuspecting urban sprawl would soon be nothing more than melted steel and mortar.

As feed after feed went dead, Rat tried to bring up other feeds so they could track what was happening.

"We have to give them time," Stickley argued.

"We just ran out of time," Purcell said. "Bring up the Power Grid?"

Rat nodded. That was easy. With a few keystrokes he had the entire North American power grid on screen. Some of it showed red, other parts green, other parts black.

"The whole of the Midwest is out," Purcell said. "So we're going to need to suck up just about every drop of juice west of the Rockies to fire Destiny at full power."

"Why now?" Stickley asked.

General Purcell pointed at the screen past Rat. "Another EM spike, and we might never get our shot. Then we're totally out of options."

General Purcell turned away from Rat and his area. Stickley followed, moving back across the room to her post.

"Contact Destiny," Purcell said to a communications officer. "Tell them to go to full power. They fire as soon as they're ready."

Rat shook his head. The man was just going to kill those left in *Virgil*, without giving them a fair chance to do what they had gone down there to do.

That wasn't right.

Rat turned and stared at the screen, at the dead area that seemed like a scar on the power grid, right in the middle of the continent.

He had to do something.

Then, staring at the grid, he knew what he could do.

He kept the news reports up on the screens for anyone who happened past, then working off a small screen directly in front of him, he dug in, his fingers flying on the keys as he went deeper and faster into the world of connected computers than he had ever gone before.

Josh sat next to Brazzleton, sweating in the heat that had now gone past one hundred degrees, even with the modifications Brazzleton and Zimsky had made earlier on the compressor. Much more and they weren't going to be able to survive in here.

He and Brazzleton were working over a large screen, doing computation after computation, trying to come up with something that would work, some way that the power they had would be enough for the task at hand.

Nothing was working.

"No, no, no," Brazzleton said, shaking his head. "Not that one."

Josh saw instantly what he meant, backed up, and stared again, running the numbers on a different scenario, a different placement of the bomb.

Zimsky sat slightly behind them, an ice pack on his jaw. He hadn't said much for the past ten minutes. But now it seemed he couldn't stay silent any longer.

"This is futile," Zimsky said. "It took me and four hundred of the world's smartest people to come up with the first plan."

"So you want to help?" Josh asked, looking back at the man.

"No," Zimsky said, "we should turn around and head home."

Brazzleton laughed. "That's not going to happen."

"Then we're going to die," Zimsky said.

Josh knew that; he was actually fine with it. They were in the Core of the planet, desperately trying to save everyone on the surface. The four of them dying was the least of the human race's worries.

He turned and went back to work, running through the figures for the bomb exploding at a higher altitude from the Inner Core–Outer Core interface.

It wasn't enough.

"Could I at least have a cigarette?"

Josh looked back at the scientist, shaking his head. Why anyone would want to smoke in a room that was over a hundred degrees was beyond Josh.

"What?" Zimsky asked at Josh's puzzled look. "You wouldn't understand. You probably jog."

Brazzleton laughed.

Suddenly Zimsky was staring at the calculations on the screen in front of Josh, his lips moving, his eyes distant.

"What?" Josh said, glancing back at the screen, then at Zimsky.

"Nothing," Zimsky said, staring at the screen, clearly lost in something he was seeing there.

Josh and Brazzleton waited, watching. Josh may hate the man, but he respected his mind, and right now that mind was working over a problem that just might save all their lives.

Finally Zimsky said, "Oh for God's sake."

"That's it," Brazzleton said, "I'm hitting him again."

"I've come up with a theory," Zimsky said, smiling at the two men.

"I want to hear it," Josh said.

"One explosion won't do it," Zimsky said. "We'll use wave interference. And if you let me have a cigarette, I'll explain."

Brazzleton glanced at Josh, who nodded.

Zimsky lit up, clearly savoring the rancid smoke.

After a moment he turned to the two men, a new focus in his eyes. Instead of complaining, it seemed to Josh that Zimsky was now back on the team.

"Think of stones in a pond," Zimsky said. "Drop one big rock, you get one big splash, and it's over."

Brazz thought he knew where this was going, but he let Zimsky continue uninterrupted.

"But drop a smaller rock, wait until the ripples weaken, then drop the next, and the next." Zimsky looked up at them, smiling. "Fluid dynamics one-oh-one. The ripples reinforce one another in geometric progression. The whole is greater than the sum of the parts."

Josh could not believe that he hadn't thought of it. "Five two hundred megaton explosions instead of just one big bang."

"Exactly," Zimsky said.

"We'll need to seed the nukes through the Core, then explode them in sequence." Josh said.

He then turned back to the computer panel and the simulations they had been running. He quickly entered in the new data, and punched start.

On the screen the explosions sent out waves, radiating, one after another, with each explosion. Slowly, on the simulation, the Core started to move, the computer showing that the theory would work.

Zimsky sat back, puffing smoke into the air, a very satisfied look on his face.

Brazzleton was smiling as well, and Josh had the same feeling. For the first time in hours, they actually had a plan.

And the planet had a chance.

chapter eighteen

B͟ECK HAD REMAINED IN THE COCKPIT WHILE THE SCIENTISTS worked on their problem. General Purcell was going to launch Destiny, but she had no intention of turning back. She just hoped they could come up with a solution before someone on the surface pushed the button or pulled the switch or however it was going to be activated.

She sat at her post as the ship dove deeper and deeper through the swirling colors of the Outer Core. Somehow, after all they had been through the last day or so, the thought of dying didn't scare her as much as it had before.

It still scared her, just not as much.

She glanced down at the temperature inside the control area. Over one hundred and three. She picked up a bottle of water and downed it, trying to let the moment clear her mind.

Not much time for that though, as the rest of her crew came barreling through the cockpit carrying all sorts of tools. They set up shop in the adjoining compartment.

She didn't want to think about what might happen if they failed. She knew enough about nuclear bombs to know that you just couldn't set one off by kicking it. But she didn't know how touchy they were otherwise. And really, at this point, didn't want to know.

Beck put *Virgil* on autopilot and poked her head through the connecting door. "So what's plan C?" she asked Josh.

"Well we drop off the nukes, blow them, then outrun the huge nuclear shockwave, penetrate the Lower Mantle, and dodge the biggest earthquake in history."

"So," Beck said, "Plan C is pretty much you winging it."

Josh smiled at her and wiped his hands on a towel. "Plan C didn't have a real long development cycle."

"The problem is," Brazzleton said, "We don't have any way to dump the bombs individually."

"That's the problem?" she asked.

"First things first," Josh said. "Let's go hot-wire some hydrogen bombs. As one does."

At that point Beck decided she had seen enough. "I'm going back to driving. I do much better driving."

She turned and headed for the control area.

Josh studied Serge's French notebook, staring at it for a moment, clearly trying to keep the sweat on his hands from smearing any of the hand-written notes. Then he said, "Cut the red wire above the circuit. No! Wait. Below."

Brazzleton looked up at him. "The red wire above or below?"

"*Au dessus* is above," Josh said. "And *au dessous* is below. Or is it the other way around?"

"I can't believe we didn't bring instructions in English for these," Zimsky said.

"They're hydrogen bombs," Brazzleton said. "They don't come with instructions."

Beck had to chuckle at them despite the circumstances. With the general about to pound the center of the Earth with a big beam, and the three stooges back there playing with hydrogen bombs, she had no doubt her life expectancy was very, very short.

The only question was, who was going to kill her first.

Josh couldn't believe they had actually finished getting the bombs ready to go. Now they just had to figure out a way to get them out there, in the right positions.

All three of them had gone back up to the control area, and had just entered when Beck pointed to the screen. "The Inner Core, gentlemen."

Beck put the ship into a smooth orbit around it, like she was piloting a shuttle.

All Josh could do was stare at the screen.

The colors of the Inner Core showing up on his display were fantastic, shifting through the rainbow, swirling and turning, some moving fast, others more slowly.

It was a light show like no other.

He was actually looking at the Core of the planet Earth.

Impossible, yet here he stood, staring at the ever-changing display of color and motion. He had no idea his screen could reproduce such vivid colors and images.

He could actually see the curve of the surface of the Core as well, and every so often what looked like a flare shot off into the Outer Core, then fell back. It was like a mini sun at the center of the Earth.

"Amazing," Zimsky said, his voice breathless. "I never thought I—"

No one said anything.

Josh knew they all felt the same way.

"The nukes are ready," he said, pulling his attention from the fantastic images of the center of the planet and back to the task at hand.

"So let's start dumping them," Beck said.

Josh looked at Brazzleton, then at Zimsky. He didn't want to be the one to tell her.

Zimsky stepped forward. "The bombs aren't built for these pressures. That's why they were in that pod. Out of that casing, they'll be crushed instantly."

Beck looked at Zimsky, then at Josh. "I'm going to assume your big brains have solved this problem."

Josh nodded, but he didn't like the solution much, and he knew Beck wouldn't either. "*Virgil*'s compartments."

"Say that again," Beck ordered.

"We put a nuke in each section of *Virgil*, and then eject the individual sections one at a time," Josh said, trying to make the entire idea sound perfectly sane. "They should stay intact long enough for the nuke to go off."

"So by the time we're done," Beck said, "we'll be left sitting on top of a nuclear-powered drill head."

All three of them nodded.

Josh had to admit that when she put it that way, it didn't sound real smart. But at this point they had no other choice that any of them could think of.

And no time left to do more thinking.

"This plan just gets better and better," Beck said.

"And better," Brazzleton said. "*Virgil*'s not designed to eject undamaged compartments."

Now that was something that Josh hadn't known.

"Any way to do it?" Zimsky asked.

"There is," Brazzleton said.

He moved over and pulled up on a screen the specs for the ship. Then, using his finger on the image, so that they could follow him, he pointed at a series of linked pistons running through the compartments.

"These are the ejection mechanisms holding the compartments in place," he said.

Josh nodded. He knew that much.

"They are all connected to one master hydraulic gear up here, like keys on a key ring."

He looked around to make sure the three of them were following him. "If we unlock that piston, it'll release all the compartments, so they can be dumped."

"And where is that master gear?" Zimsky asked, right before Josh could.

"In the crawlspace we used to get out earlier," Brazzleton said, pointing to the impeller area on the specs.

All three of them stood there in silence. It suddenly felt like the room got a lot hotter. All Josh could think about was how it was out of their reach. How a simple switch was going to mean the end of the world.

"What the hell is it doing in there?" Zimsky asked.

Brazzleton defended his creation. "I built the damn ship in three months. I didn't think I'd be intentionally sabotaging it."

Josh knew what had to happen. They could not let something like this stop them. "One of us has to go out there."

"That crawlspace has Core fluid passing through it. At nine thousand degrees," Beck said.

"Flush it with liquid nitrogen again," Josh said. He knew they had some, and he knew what it would mean for the temperature inside the ship, but they had no choice. Someone had to go out there.

"Nine thousand degrees," Zimsky said, shaking his head. "Even if we shut down the impeller, cool the chamber and these suits hold up . . ."

Josh completed the thought. "Whoever goes in that crawlspace is not coming back."

Beck looked at him, yet she didn't argue. At this point in the mission, there was no arguing with anything. They were doing what had to be done.

Brazzleton turned and rummaged in the tool box, took a roll of wire out, snipped off three pieces and then, with his back turned, mixed them up before turning around.

"No wire for Beck," Josh said. "This bus only has one driver."

Zimsky and Brazzleton stared at each other.

"Try your luck, Zimsky," Brazzleton said.

"Will it be luck, Brazzleton?" Zimsky said, reaching for a wire.

Josh reached out and took one at the same time. "Together," he said.

They drew. Both wires were the same length.

Josh couldn't tell if he was disappointed, or elated that he wasn't going to die in the next minute. He had accepted that he was going to die down here, in the center of the planet, but knowing exactly when was another matter.

Brazzleton held up what looked to be the short straw. "Well, I'd better—"

Zimsky grabbed Brazzleton's wrist and held it.

"Please," Zimsky said, "this is childish."

Brazzleton sighed and opened his hand. The wire in his hand unbent to the same length as the others.

"I thought you'd be happy," Brazzleton said to Zimsky.

"Not at the expense of you treating us like fools," Zimsky said.

"He's right," Josh said. "Why do you get dibs on being the hero?"

"Because it's my damn ship," Brazzleton said.

"Oh, that makes perfect sense," Zimsky said, clearly disgusted.

Josh was starting to feel the same way.

"Look," Brazzleton said, "I've got nothing but *Virgil*. I can't let it fail, not after twenty years ."

He paused and then looked at Beck, then back at Zimsky. "What's worth dying for? You asked that question, didn't you? This ship. Building it instead of imagining it. If this ship needs blood, it's going to be mine."

217

Zimsky opened his mouth to say something, then closed it, staring at Brazzleton.

Josh had nothing he could add to that either. The subject was closed. Brazzleton was going to go unlock the manual controls to allow them to separate the ship. And in so doing, he was going to die.

"Now help me get into that damn suit," Brazzleton said, turning and heading for where the suits were kept.

Beck touched Josh's shoulder and turned and went back to her controls.

Less than a minute later they had Brazzleton in his suit. He moved over and crouched near the access panel that they had come into the ship through. It dropped down into the impeller area. Josh could feel the heat radiating up through the hole, making the control room even hotter than it already was. And as soon as they flushed the impeller area, it was going to get even warmer.

Brazz turned to the others as he crouched at the top of the crawlspace. "Good to go. Josh, Beck, I'm real proud to have known ya."

"Helluva boat you built, Brazz," Beck said. She was doing better than Josh who couldn't even speak.

Brazz nodded proudly at the compliment, and started down the ladder.

Zimsky, who had his back turned, clearly trying to

keep himself under control, turned back to face Brazzleton for one last time.

"Brazz," Zimsky said.

But Brazzleton had already reached the bottom of the ladder, and didn't respond.

"Edward!" Zimsky said, calling out Brazzleton's first name.

"Yes, Conrad," Brazzleton said, reappearing momentarily.

"You're right," Zimsky said, "it is *your* ship. But I have to tell you, I wish to God, it was *our* ship."

Brazzleton stared up at Zimsky, then nodded and moved to one side, allowing Josh to close the airlock.

Over the comm link, Brazzleton said, "The chamber's empty. Do it."

Josh turned and stared at Beck. The man had just sealed his own death sentence.

Beck punched the button.

On the screen showing the impeller area, Brazzleton dropped into sight.

His scream echoed through the comm link as he hit the hot air, but Josh didn't dare pull his headset off.

The metal wrench in his hands melted, and his gloves started to smoke.

"Brazz, hold on," Josh shouted.

Brazzleton moved the one step to the panel and opened it. Inside was a large metal piston made out of the same stuff the rest of the outside of the ship was made of.

Josh could not believe how hot it must be in there. Brazzleton's suit was catching fire. He must have been in agony.

Brazzleton, his gloves burning, reached up and pulled the piston out, then turned it and pushed it back into place.

"Manual override is complete," Beck said, staring at her panel where a green light had switched to red. "Brazz, we can get you out of there."

"Start the impeller," Brazzleton said, his voice barely loud enough to hear.

Josh looked at Beck. Both of them knew that Brazzleton was right. They had to start the impeller. He wasn't going to survive. His suit was now in full flames, his faceplate starting to melt.

"Good-bye, Brazz," Beck said, her hand over the control that would start the impellers and flush hot core fluid through the impeller area.

Josh couldn't let her do this one alone. She had made the right decision with Serge, but there was no telling what two similar decisions would do to her.

He stepped over and put his hand under hers. Her hand wouldn't be the one to hit the button and kill their teammate this time.

She nodded, and together they pushed down on the switch.

There was a faint whine of the impeller starting up.

On the screen, Brazzleton, his suit on fire, reached out and patted the side of his ship.

It was a pat of love.

A moment later core fluid roared into the chamber and Brazzleton was incinerated instantly.

chapter nineteen

COLONEL CHILDS HAD LEFT THE COMM LINK OPEN TO DEEP-Earth Control, hoping that if they heard the progress *Virgil* was making, they might hold off firing Destiny.

Now, as Rat worked, digging deeper and deeper into the computers that controlled things in this country and around the world, he heard Brazzleton die.

Rat couldn't believe the sacrifices those crew members on *Virgil* were making. It was the least he could do to try to let them have a real chance. He couldn't let General Purcell just kill them. Not after all this.

Rat didn't let his fingers slow down as behind him on Stickley's control desk a phone rang.

General Purcell walked over and picked it up and listened. Around him the control room was silent, everyone seeming to hold their breaths.

After a moment the general said, "All right. Initiate the firing sequence."

"Sir!" Stickley said.

Rat paused and turned to watch.

General Purcell hung up and pointed to an image of the national power grid that he had had Rat display on a big screen. Sections of it were blinking; a few others were out completely.

"This is the last shot we get, Stick," the general said.

"Damn you!" Stickley said.

Rat doubted there wasn't a person in the control area that didn't echo those same feelings about the general right now.

"Damn me?" Purcell asked, staring ahead. "Too late."

Rat would have to agree with that as well.

He turned back to his board and kept working, faster than he had been working before. He had to give *Virgil* a chance.

Josh could not believe how heavy a hydrogen bomb could be. Using a small cart, he and Zimsky had managed to drag, pull, and lift the first bomb back to the last compartment, and now had it in position.

They managed to get the bomb off the cart, and the cart back out the door before Beck said over the comm link, "Approaching the first drop-off point. We gotta be accurate to the second here, boys. Hope we're up to it."

"Hey, we're seven foot high and bulletproof, remember?" Josh said, as he wiped sweat off his face with a towel, and then tossed the cloth aside.

"Drop in fifty-five seconds," Beck said.

Zimsky held up a stopwatch and pointed at Josh. "Ready?"

"Ready?" Josh said, making sure the bomb's timer mechanism was open in front of him.

"Now," Zimsky said.

Josh hit the start switch on the bomb's preset timer, made sure the first second ticked off, then followed Zimsky at a full run for the door.

"Clear!" Beck shouted through the comm link.

A moment later the door started down, slamming hard when it hit the bottom.

"Section away," Beck said.

Zimsky and Josh were at a full run, pulling the bomb cart behind them, heading to get the next bomb into place in the next compartment.

This was going to be the hardest workout Josh had ever gotten, that much he was sure. He just hoped Zimsky was up to it.

Rat was almost in. Almost.

For the last five minutes, every time he thought he was through, something stopped him.

Encrypted! came up twice, Access Denied a half

dozen times. But he was the best there was. Those words only challenged him, made him more focused.

Then, suddenly, one of the screens showed real words, then command menus appeared.

He laughed. "Your kung fu is not strong," he said to the site he had been trying to hack.

"Full power to Destiny in fifteen seconds," Rat heard someone say behind him.

"May God have mercy on us all," General Purcell said.

Around Rat the entire command area was silent except for the reports of sections being released from *Virgil*, each containing a bomb.

Rat just couldn't understand it. The three of them left down there were killing themselves to save the planet, and yet General Purcell wanted to kill them first.

That wasn't going to happen. Not if Rat had anything to say about it.

"Five. Four. Three. Two. One."

The countdown to firing Destiny went off like a clock ticking, but Rat knew now that it signaled nothing.

He smiled as over the comm link with the Destiny project he heard the words, "Where the hell's our juice gone?"

Around Deep-Earth Command a snicker started, whispers filled the once silent room.

Over the comm link from Destiny, another engineer said, "It says here, Coney Island."

That broke up the entire command center.

Rat turned to look at General Purcell, who clearly was angry.

"How long will it take to get it back on line?!" Purcell demanded as he picked up the ringing phone.

"Then get to it!"

He slammed the phone back into its cradle and everyone around the control area pretended to be busy. The general knew who was responsible, but he never would be able to prove it. He headed toward Rat's work station.

Rat quickly brought up an old game of Pong and started playing it.

A moment later the general stood behind him.

Rat glanced around. "Anything I can do for you, General?"

The general started to open his mouth, then waved his hand and turned back to the command area.

Rat just smiled. Now it was up to *Virgil*. Now they had a chance. He just hoped they wouldn't let him, and the entire world, down.

Josh stared at the next to last bomb they were going to have to jettison. He and Zimsky were in the living compartment, the only piece of the ship left other than the navigation center.

Josh could never remember working so hard.

Zimsky was sweating so hard, it was running down his face. Josh felt the same way.

"These are the last ones, Beck," he said into his headset.

Zimsky wiped off his face, then stood, staring at the bomb, the faraway look on his face. Josh knew that look didn't bode well, since there was clearly something bothering Zimsky, and had been now for two bombs.

"Beck," Zimsky said into his comm link, "what's the energy propagation wavelength for the Core fluid?"

Josh instantly knew where he was heading. They hadn't checked that one detail. They had been only working off the assumption that Core fluid with the same weight and mass as matter on the surface would have the same properties.

"You should be able to get it from the Impeller sonics," Zimsky said to Beck. "Just multiply up by a thousand."

There was a pause, them Beck said, "Two-point-seven thousand kilometers."

Zimsky suddenly looked like the heat had finally made him sick.

"Foolish, foolish man," Zimsky said to himself. "It's not enough! The last bomb is not enough! Fluid dynamics 102! We need a larger bomb to complete the waveform. A forty goddam percent larger bomb!"

"That will take another six or seven pounds of pluto-nium," Josh said, the feeling of dread building in his stomach. He knew enough about fluid dynamics to know that Zimsky was more than likely right. "Where the hell . . ."

He was interrupted as an energy flare broke close to *Virgil.*

The ship suddenly lurched to the right.

Josh was tossed against the bulkhead, hitting his shoulder hard. And then, before he could move, the bomb on its cart, rolled toward him, pinning him under it.

The pain against his thighs and chest was incredible.

Zimsky scrambled over and tried to push the cart back up the slope that was holding it against Josh.

Josh did his best to help, but nothing seemed to be budging that cart. It was just too heavy, and with the ship tipped the way it was, there was no pushing it.

"I can't hold us on course! Ejecting compartment in fifty seconds," Beck said.

Zimsky and Josh both pushed as hard as they could, fighting to get the bomb to move just a few inches so that Josh could squeeze out.

Finally, Zimsky started to back away. "I'm very sorry dear boy, truly am . . ."

"Disengaging fail-safes," Beck said.

Josh reached out with one hand and grabbed his

headset. He had an idea what might work, at least free him enough to get out.

"Beck. Nose down!" he said.

Virgil turned downward, and the bomb instantly rolled away from Josh. He bounced off a wall and right into Zimsky, pinning him under the cart and tipping the bomb over.

Josh pulled himself to his feet as Zimsky screamed in pain. He got to Zimsky's side and tried to push the bomb off of him. It was clear the scientist's legs were broken, and he was pinned completely.

"Ejecting that compartment in ten," Beck said.

"Go!" Zimsky said, pushing Josh away. "Go."

Josh ignored him.

"Go!" Zimsky shouted. "Now!"

Zimsky reached out and shoved Josh hard through the closing door into the last intact compartment. Before he could react, the door sealed shut behind him.

The compartment separated from *Virgil* with a clank.

Over the comm link Zimsky shouted, "Keyes. The reactor!"

Then the link was broken and Zimsky was gone.

Josh looked over at the last bomb and realized what Zimsky had meant. And he didn't have much time to make it happen.

He quickly set the bomb's timer, then at a full run he headed for the EVA suits hanging near the entrance.

"What's happening back there?" Beck asked in his comm link as he quickly put on his suit, gloves, and helmet.

"Zimsky's dead," Josh said. "And I have to make a few adjustments for the last bomb. Stay in position."

"Can't I help you?" Beck asked.

"I need you there to make sure the last compartment is released on time."

"Understood," she said.

He took a deep breath and went into the reactor area of the main section of *Virgil*. It was a closed space, very tight, like a small elevator. For a moment his claustrophobia kicked up, and all he wanted to do was get out of there, be anywhere else.

He pushed the fear, and the feelings, aside. He moved to the cover of the reactor and opened it in one motion, looking inside.

Around him all the power dropped to standby levels as the reactor did an emergency power-down.

"What's happening?" Beck asked.

"Stay there," Josh said.

On the radiation monitors the dials were high, but still in the green. But the temperature monitors for the reactor were off the scale. He doubted even the suit and gloves would protect him from those levels of heat. At this point he didn't have any choice.

He made sure the reactor had completely powered

down, then reached in and grabbed the shielded reactor core.

The pain of the burning through his gloves made him scream, but he held on.

He moved out of the reactor area and back into the last compartment, somehow, even though it was burning his hands through the gloves, holding onto the reactor core.

"Ejecting the last compartment," Beck said.

Josh put the plutonium beside the bomb, made sure the timer on the bomb was still going, then turned and dove for the closing door.

Somehow, he made it through.

He lay there on the deck of the cockpit panting, not wanting to think about how badly burned his hands were.

"You dumped the reactor core," Beck said.

"Had to . . ." Josh panted. "Build the blast . . . sorry."

Beck cradled his head. "Ssh. You did good. It's okay."

chapter twenty

JOSH HAD LET BECK HELP HIM OUT OF HIS SUIT AND PUT PAIN-killer on his hands. They were bad, but not so bad that he couldn't use them if he needed to. There wasn't much of a chance he was going to need to, however.

Around them the control room was almost dark. The emergency power had just about drained away. What really bothered Josh more than anything was that he was going to die before he found out if all their work had saved the planet. That just didn't seem fair.

Both of them were in their chairs, Beck at the controls, turned so that she could see him. Why they had gone back to those positions, he had no idea. Habit died hard, even when a person was dying, it seemed.

As the oxygen levels got lower in the control area, he

was discovering that more and more things seemed to be funny.

"One minute to the last detonation," Beck said, glancing at her watch. "Three until the blast wave hits us."

"Damn," Josh said, wiping sweat from his face. "I was hoping we'd suffocate to death first." He had no idea how little oxygen was left or hot the temperature was in there at the moment, and he was glad they didn't have enough power to find out.

"Well, let's look on the bright side," Beck said. "We might get our faces on a postage stamp."

"Not if no one ever knows what we did," Josh said. He figured that since they were going to die, no one would ever hear about the things that Zimsky and Brazzleton had done to make it all happen.

He shook his head and then smiled at her. Even covered in sweat and about to die, she was still the most beautiful thing he had ever seen. Never had he felt like that about a woman. And now it was too late.

"I should have kissed you that day on the launch pad," he said.

"Yeah," Beck said, pretending to be angry at him. "You should have."

As he started to stand and move toward her chair, he happened to glance back at Brazzleton's empty station.

Suddenly he had an idea that just might save them.

233

Brazzleton had explained that the material he called Unobtainiam converted heat to power to help reinforce the hull.

"Beck, Beck," he said, just staring ahead.

"What?" she said, looking at him like the oxygen had completely left his brain.

"What could you do if I got you enough power to fire the impeller?"

She looked at him like he was totally nuts. "From where?"

Josh pointed. "The heat of the core. We're at nine thousand degrees! Unobtainium converts heat to energy. This whole damn ship is like a big, old solar panel!"

He turned away from her and headed for the tool box.

Beck swung back to face forward in her chair, and did her best to check out the systems in the lower power mode. "Whatever you're doing—do it faster!" she said.

Ignoring the pain in his hands, Josh went to the power connectors leading into the reactor, yanked two loose, and hooked up some loose wire to them, then ran that wire to one of the contacts on one of the hull plates.

He carefully hooked up the first one, then shoved the second into place, causing sparks to fly out around him. That stuff was really putting out the juice at these temperatures and pressure. He would need to be careful. The last thing he and Beck needed now was for him to get electrocuted.

The wire didn't stay on the first try, but it did on the second, and the lights came up around them.

"Not enough!" Beck shouted from behind him. "I got life support and cooling and sensors, but not enough to start the engines and lasers."

"Damn," he said.

He quickly hooked up two more wires to the main input cables, and then strung them along to the next hull panel, again managing to not get himself shocked as he hooked it into the circuit of a second wall unit.

Sparks flew everywhere, and he ducked most of them. The wires held in position, more than likely fused.

"Got it!" Beck said. "Get back in your seat. The wave is about on top of us!"

Josh ran back and tried his best to get buckled in, even with his burnt hands. The big screen in front of them showed the wave coming at the ship as a big ripple. Just when they thought they'd stay dead in the water the ultrasonic spun up and the impellers started to slowly turn. If the wave hit them just right . . .

"Come back, baby," Beck said, as she ran through the ultrasonic and impeller start-up sequence, cutting all the corners she could. "Come back . . ."

Then the roar of a tidal wave of energy descended on *Virgil*. It was now or never.

"Get ready to pull a few g's," Beck said.

"Never been readier," Josh said.

He sat back as the wave slowly took them and fired them forward, shoving them through the liquid rock faster than he would have ever thought possible.

To his amazement, Josh was enjoying the ride.

Beck wasn't enjoying anything yet. She was far too busy trying to keep them alive.

Rat was stunned as suddenly *Virgil* was back on the screen. He had thought them dead and had been sitting there cussing himself for stopping Destiny, then suddenly *Virgil* was back.

And from the sensor readings, moving faster than should have ever been possible.

At that moment a huge quake rocked the base, sending everything bouncing that wasn't tied down.

Rat had made sure that all his computers were secured when he set them up, so the only thing he lost was an old bottle of Mountain Dew.

He rode the quake, his fingers pulling up screen after screen as he worked to find out the extent of what was happening to them, tapping into every available earthquake sensing sight he had on line. What he found just astounded him.

"What's the center of this quake?" General Purcell shouted from behind him.

"It's everywhere," Rat said, laughing. "It's one big shock wave,"

His fingers flew over the keys, flashing images of New York on the screen as the buildings rocked. Then a picture of the Golden Gate, as it swayed and then settled back into position.

All around the world, the shock waves moved.

Suddenly the wave was past the base, and everyone in Deep-Earth Control was talking at the same time.

On the big screen, the blip that was *Virgil* still sped through the Earth's Core, heading at full speed for the Mantle.

"Stay with us," Rat said, making sure that all the computer systems that could were tracking the ship. "Stay with us."

Suddenly one of the technicians shouted, "They're in the Mantle.

"Where are they headed?" General Purcell demanded.

"Colonel Childs found a space between some tectonic plates," someone said.

"Damn, you are good," Josh said, holding on with his burnt hands as Beck fought the ship first one direction, then back.

"Shut up and let me drive," she said.

Without all the segments attached to *Virgil*, she had a much more maneuverable ship, but still it was taking all the skill of a fighter pilot to keep them alive and moving forward. Especially at the speed they were moving. Josh couldn't believe the impellers could take up and spit out material that fast. Of course, a lot of their speed was also because the material around them was moving as well.

"Shortcut!" she said.

Josh watched on the map as she took them into a magma chute that went straight up toward the surface. It was like a hang glider catching a great updraft. To keep control she circled a little, but mostly she just let the flow carry them.

"We're heading up between two closing plates," Josh said, studying the images ahead. "You know that, don't you?"

"I do," Beck said. "But I'm hoping we can get through before they close."

"So do I," Josh said. "So do I."

On the big screen, as the dot that indicated *Virgil* worked its way up between the two huge masses of rock, it suddenly went dark.

Rat worked his keyboards, trying to get anything to come back.

Any sensor reading.

Any signal on any wavelength.

Nothing.

Around him in Deep-Earth Control the other technicians were silent. None of them could believe that after all this, *Virgil* was gone. Something must have happened to their comm link.

Rat worked nonstop until a hand was placed on his shoulder. Stickley was getting some last minute info as she stood behind him. She nodded her head and the technician moved off.

"General, Rat—let's take a walk," she said.

Rat stood, and with the general and Stickley, he headed out the door and into the cool night air of the Utah desert. Hundreds and hundreds of other base personnel were out there, some sitting, most just standing, staring upward.

Overhead, where every night for weeks there had been dancing northern lights, there was now mostly stars. There was still a few remains of the dancing colors, but as he watched, even they faded and were gone.

The crisp stars of the desert night returned, filling the night sky as they should.

Rat sat heavily on the ground, the relief so great that his legs wouldn't hold him anymore. The grief for the lost crew of *Virgil* made him weep.

"They did it," Stickley said, patting the top of his head. Thanks to you, they got the chance they needed."

Rat just sat there, staring up at the sky.

This time the human race had been saved. This time.

chapter twenty-one

JOSH SAT BESIDE BECK IN THE DARK, WATCHING AS EVEN THE
lights on a few buttons faded and were gone. He clicked
on a flashlight he had dug out of storage before the
lights went all the way out. He propped the light on his
dead control board, shining it on the ceiling over them
to allow them to at least see each other.

"Where'd our power go?" Beck asked, shaking her
head.

"We were powered by the heat of the core," Josh
said. "It's stone cold down here."

Beck had done a masterful job of getting them out of
the Earth alive. She had managed to steer *Virgil*
through places Josh was sure they wouldn't fit, and
cover a distance in six hours that had taken them over
a day to cover going the other direction.

The lava vent they had come up through had spit them out at the bottom of the Pacific Ocean, fairly close to where they had gone in. And since they were powered by heat, the moment they emerged into the cold ocean, they lost their power.

All of it.

"Well," Josh said, starting to get cold for the first time in over a day, "look at the bright side. At least we won't boil to death."

"You always look on the bright side?" Beck asked, giving her dead control board one last look.

"Always," Josh said, smiling at her.

Beck spun back in her chair to face Josh. She was less optimistic of their chances as she ticked off the specifics of their situation. "Okay, let's assess," she said. "We've got no communications, we're probably eight hundred feet down but we might as well be eight hundred miles." Josh nodded in agreement. "We're in an unobtanium cigar tube with the sonar signature of a rock," Beck continued. "We've got just enough power to burp the ultrasonics, but no one's going to be listening on those frequencies anyway. And nobody even knows we're alive."

Josh looked at her, then said, "Okay, give me a minute on this one."

She laughed, and the sound was beautiful, even in the tomb they called a ship. Somehow, he had to figure out a way to get them to the surface, to keep hearing that laugh for a long time to come.

Suddenly, it dawned on him. He knew exactly how he could do it.

Rat had figured out exactly where *Virgil* would have come through the ocean floor. Then, somehow, he convinced General Purcell that he was right, and there was still a chance they were alive.

The moment Purcell heard that, and looked at the information Rat had put together, he ordered them onto a helicopter, and twelve long hours later, they were on the deck of the U.S.S. Aircraft Carrier *Abraham Lincoln* as it headed for the location Rat had picked.

By that point the search was already underway, but no one really knew what they were looking for.

Rat sat with the general and the carrier captain studying the GPS readouts. As much as he wanted to hear good news, the general had faced too many battles and endured the loss of too many soldiers to hold out false hope.

"Mr. Finch," he said to Rat in stoic military fashion, "they have no way of contacting us, their life support—"

Rat wouldn't listen. Somehow, there had to be a way to locate them, even though they would have no power to signal.

"Sir," one technician said, after saluting the general, "the sub sonar's picked up something."

The captain turned up the speakers and there was a staticky whine. For the first time in days, Purcell allowed himself to feel hopeful.

"That's just a pod of whales," the captain said. "They're way off their usual path, but it's not uncommon since that, what was it called—orbital wobble?"

The general nodded. "Yes. That's what they called it."

Rat shook his head at the continued stupidity of the government. Then he went over and stood with his back to a window, staring at the room full of sophisticated sonar and electronic equipment, trying to figure out what was bothering him.

Something about those whales.

Then it hit him.

Whales.

"Of course it's whales!" Rat shouted, making the technicians in the room and General Purcell turn to look at him.

"Josh is pulsing the ultrasonic beam. It's super–low frequency sound waves, so when he pulses it to get our attention . . ."

"It attracts whales!" the general said, jumping to order the rescue craft to go back to that pod of whales.

"Find the whale sounds," Rat said to the sonar tech.

The young kid nodded, his fingers moving over the

keyboard fast, showing that he was good at more than just running sonar. Then, without asking, the kid found the whale sounds and cleared them out, leaving only one sound.

The low hum of an ultrasonic drill, pulsing on and off.

Rat had never heard such a wonderful sound before. And for a moment he thought the general might actually hug him.

The helicopter pilot tipped his craft sideways and looked for a pod of whales. At the co-ordinates radioed from the *Lincoln*, there was nothing but the slightly choppy sea.

"Nothing yet," he reported into his communications link with the ship. The sound of the sonar pulsing filled his ears, as if he was getting closer to the source. But he knew they were all running out of time.

Then to his left he saw movement. A whale broke the surface, spraying a fine mist into the air.

Then another.

And another.

"Hold on," he said into his microphone. "I'm seeing something." He veered a bit to the right and looked down.

He banked hard and within a few seconds he was hovering over the whales. Only a few broke the surface, but from what he could tell on his sonar, there were a lot of them just beneath the waves.

"I'm seeing whales here," he reported. "But . . ." he paused, not sure exactly what else he was seeing.

On his sonar screen a large, rock-like object appeared below the whales in about seven hundred feet of water. But it was too smooth, too perfect to be a rock, and it was exactly the right shape.

"Wait a minute," the pilot said. "We're getting something on the sonar. There's something down there!"

The first bang on the hull had sent Josh and Beck both jumping. Josh had begun to doubt that his idea had worked, that no one would think to look where there were whales.

Then there was more banging, more scraping, and the sounds of lines being attached to the outside of the hull. If he had more energy, more room, and wasn't so darned cold, he would stand up and dance.

After a few very long, very cold minutes, the nose of the ship tipped upward. Both of them scrambled to hook in their seat belts, and then they just lay back in the dim light.

"I told you," Josh said, after the ship had been pulled completely off the bottom and the scraping noises had stopped, "pulsing the ultrasonics would work."

"Do you ever get tired of being right?" Beck asked, smiling at him.

Josh looked at her. As the renewed hope of their survival underscored the despair of their losses, he answered "Yes."

By the time the big ship had reached the scene, the ocean surface was a madhouse. Rat could see at least a dozen Zodiacs on the water, filled with divers in wetsuits. Three helicopters churned the water's surface, all with lines extending down into the water.

And beyond that, the whales still hovered around, seeming unperturbed by all the activity.

The deep-water rescue experts had determined the best way to get *Virgil* to the surface was to use the winches on the helicopters coupled with the floatation devices being attached to the craft by a team of divers. It was their only chance to raise the ship in time to save the crew.

And along the way up to the surface more and more flotation collars would be fitted to *Virgil*, to ensure it didn't sink back to the bottom, and also give the helicopters help in the lift.

Never had Rat imagined a so perfectly timed bit of chaos before. Everyone seemed to know exactly what they were doing, and so far, everything was going smoothly.

Divers were constantly in and out of the water as the roar of the helicopters drowned out all other noise in the immediate area. Rat couldn't imagine how loud it must be on the surface of the water below those hovering monsters.

The discovery of the *Virgil* had excited everyone, but congratulations would be withheld until the ship was on the surface and the hatch opened. Only then would they know if their efforts had truly succeeded.

"So what's next for you?" Josh asked Beck, turning so he could see her face in the dim light. Around them the slow movement of *Virgil* toward the surface gave him hope, but until he saw daylight and breathed fresh air again, he couldn't completely relax.

"A shower," Beck said, shrugging. "Then back to NASA, I guess. You?"

"Deep dish pepperoni pizza, green pepper, onions, extra mushrooms," Josh said, feeling his stomach shake at the very thought. "Then a shower. Then back to the classroom."

"NASA could use a few good men, you know," Beck said, her voice soft.

"Yeah," Josh said, laughing, "unfortunately, so could my freshman geology students."

The silence in *Virgil* seemed to grow between them as they retreated into their own thoughts. It was still cold, but not as bad, and the air seemed thin, but still breathable.

Outside, the noise against the hull had stopped for

the moment, but Josh could still feel that *Virgil* was being pulled upward.

"You know what pisses me off?" Beck said.

Josh stared at her, waiting for her to go on.

"Bob, Serge, Brazz, Zimsky. No one's ever going to know what they did, or why they died. Are they?"

Josh knew she was right. No one would know about this mission, about any of this. . . . "Unless," he said, a devilish grin crossing his face, "this all got out on the Internet somehow."

They stared at each other. Beck's military discipline would never allow her to leak such a story, and Josh's security clearances would surely be compromised if he said anything.

"Yeah . . . that's unthinkable," Beck said, straight-faced and instantly committed to the unspoken plan.

"Yeah," Josh said.

Rat stood at the side of the ship, watching the water churn from the downwash of the three helicopters hovering overhead. It seemed they had been at the rescue for hours, yet his watch said it had been only twenty minutes.

One man in a Zodiac made a motion with his hand and twelve divers hit the water in almost perfect unison. They pulled large yellow floatation devices as they swam toward an area directly in the center of the three cables extending from the helicopters.

Then slowly, almost as if it didn't want to come back to the light of day, *Virgil* broke the surface of the water. Its skin was scarred and burnt-looking, yet it was the most beautiful thing that Rat had ever seen.

Everyone on the ship started cheering, then the cheers slowly died off as the divers scrambled to put even more of the yellow flotation collars on *Virgil*, bringing up the entire ship and making sure it would stay afloat.

Then, one by one, the helicopters were released, everyone making sure *Virgil* remained afloat before they were turned away.

The final helicopter held on as three divers moved to the top of the ship. The wind from the propellers made their scramble over the metal an even more daunting task. Then, after the longest few seconds of Rat's life, one of the men straddling the top of *Virgil* turned toward the ship and waved.

From the communications area Rat heard the cheer start and he knew, without asking, that Beck and Josh were alive.

Venice, California . . . One Week Later

No one in the Internet cafe really noticed when the man in a long coat entered. He had several files under one arm and a hat pulled down to shade his sunglassed eyes.

The computers were almost all in use, but two stations were empty, one near the back.

The man in the coat moved up to the counter, ordered an iced mocchachino with extra whipped cream, and headed to a secluded station far from the window.

He dropped the pile of folders on the desk. Each was marked "FOR YOUR EYES ONLY" or "TOP SECRET." He opened the first folder and took a sip of his mocchachino, contemplating where to begin his work. He frowned. Something was wrong. He reached into his long coat and found the missing piece of his puzzle. Throwing the Hot Pockets onto the desk, he was now ready to begin.

Then the man named Rat cracked his knuckles, and with the flourish and intensity of a virtuoso pianist began to "play" the keyboard with vigor.

"World, meet Destiny. Destiny, meet world."

On the screen the addresses of the world's major news sources started to appear. CNN. *New York Times. Pravda. Le Monde.*

And with each new address, Rat smiled a little more.

Two days later, Rat flipped from one major news feed to another, smiling. He had made it happen. Destiny was no longer a deep, dark secret. He had known why it had to be in the beginning, why he had had to stonewall and control the entire Internet. But now what those brave souls had done was rightfully out in the open.

On a French station they were praising Serge, the respected French scientist who had died saving the planet Earth. They were talking about giving him the highest honor ever given in France to a soldier.

Rat had no doubt that Serge deserved it.

Rat flipped to CNN. There a news anchor was giving the background into Brazz's life, his inventions and his heroic death as his greatest creation saved everyone else.

On MSNBC, they were replaying the president's speech. In the speech the president had promised to honor not only the dead, but Josh and Beck as well. The president said they would all be treated as national heroes.

Rat knew, without a doubt, that they were heroes. And now the entire world knew it, and would honor those who went to the center of the Earth to save everyone.

That was as it should be.